Violet Black

& the Curse of Camp Coldwater

By Kevin M. Folliard

For the kids who never look back…

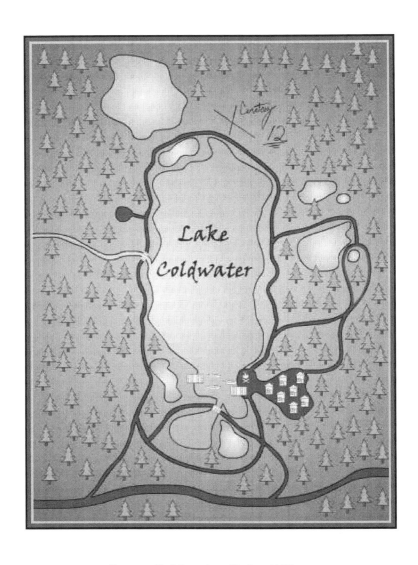

Camp Coldwater Rule #13:

Always hike with a buddy! ☺

ACKNOWLEDGMENTS

Special thanks to my wonderful network of writer friends who helped me refine this story.

1

"Please don't make me, Dad!" Violet pleaded from the passenger seat.

"It's decided, Violet. You're not spending any more summers chasing the paranormal," her father replied.

"But if you take me with you, I'll study the whole time," Violet insisted. "I'll never even leave the hotel."

Her father adjusted the sun visor. "All the inns we'll be visiting are haunted to the roof. You know that."

"They can't be as bad as where I'm going."

"Do you remember that summer in Cairo when you were eight years old? The Pharaoh's curse?"

"That was fun. I learned hieroglyphics." Violet pointed her finger matter-of-factly.

"How about that outbreak of Lycanthropy in the London countryside when you were nine?"

Violet dismissed him with a wave of her hand. "Werewolves-schmerewolves! I got to hang out with Grandma that summer."

Her father's eyes remained fixed on the road. "What about that poltergeist in Boston?"

"Not as bad as where I'm going now."

"The wailing banshees of County Mayo?"

"Not. As. Bad."

"Dracula's Castle."

"Was *so* much fun! That cult guy there . . ." Violet wavered her hand pensively. "Eh, not as fun. But still, *this* is worse!"

Her father bit his lip. "What about the time my research assistant was possessed by that Babylonian god?"

"Not as bad, Daddy. You had that under control. I knew you did the whole time." Violet smiled warmly, in case he was watching out of the corner of his eye.

Her father failed to suppress a flattered grin. "Um. Yes, well . . . what about the time--"

"Dad!" Violet crossed her arms. She watched the gray-green forest rush by out the window. "Nothing is worse than *summer camp*. Nothing."

The gentle hum of the SUV's engine and the steady blow of air conditioning filled the silence. A big bug splattered against the windshield. Violet's father spritzed it with fluid, and its yellow guts smeared the glass.

"Well," her father said, "Wisconsin is beautiful, and the brochure sounded lovely. Lots of activities. Getting in touch with nature--"

"It's against *my* nature." Violet twisted her seatbelt around her wrist. "I have more eclectic interests than most kids. Very dignified like my father. I shouldn't be taken out of my element, you know?"

"You really ought to be spending your summers," he sighed, "with other children."

"I'm *not* a child. I'm thirteen."

"Then you should spend your summers with other *thirteen*-year-olds," he said.

"I want to spend them with you," she muttered.

They drove in silence for a moment. "It's only six weeks, love," he finally said.

"It's only *forever*."

"Don't be dramatic."

"When you were thirteen, you would have *died* if your parents sent you to some dilapidated old camp full of jocks and Neanderthals."

He laughed. "I was fascinated by anthropology at your age. I would have survived. You will too."

"You know I'll haunt you if I don't," Violet kidded. But then she remembered she was angry. "Daddy, please turn this car around."

"Spoiled rotten. Where did I go wrong?" He shook his head.

"I'm serious."

"It's paid for, Violet. I'm sorry. This is happening. You'd better start making the best of it."

Violet wracked her brain, desperate for some answer to her father's final word. But deep down she knew it was checkmate. Professor Dorian Black wasn't budging this time. She had been trying to convince him for weeks, and it was time to surrender. Yet it wasn't having to go to summer camp that hurt. It was the total rejection from her only family. Daddy-daughter summer adventures were over.

"I hate you," she blurted out.

"You do not."

"The only reason you're doing this is because you don't think you can concentrate on your work if I'm around. But I can take care of myself. You just don't trust me."

Violet's father pulled to the side of the road and parked at the edge of the woods. He massaged the bridge of his nose and closed his eyes for a moment, then turned to give her his undivided attention. "Listen carefully, Violet. Because I'm not repeating this again, and I refuse to part angry with my only child. I trust you most explicitly. You're a brilliant, responsible, young woman, and you have never failed to make me proud. But we've lost your mother. My work is dangerous. And I refuse to lose you too."

Outside, a crow's caw grated deep in the North Woods.

"Do we understand one another?"

Violet wiped a tear from under her eye. She nodded. *Great,* she thought. *On top of all this, he's playing the Mom guilt card.* She had no case here. Not now. She would be doing the same thing in his place.

"Are you going to give me any more grief?" he asked.

"No."

"All right then." He shifted gears and pulled back onto the road. After another ten minutes of staring into dark gray trees, she managed to work up her humility. "I love you, Daddy. I'm sorry."

"I love you always and forever," he said. Violet was taken aback. He hadn't said that to her in years. It had always been the last thing he told her each night after he tucked her into bed. But Violet hadn't needed tucking-in quite a while.

"You'll make friends, sweetheart. You're a charming girl."

Violet forced a smile. Making herself known was never a problem. Making friends was iffier. "There's going to be sports, and hiking, and all sorts of things I'm not good at." She shrugged.

"Well, you know a few good ghost stories," he said. "Impress them around the campfire."

She nodded. Maybe her dad didn't understand that being the creepy, weird, ghost girl was guaranteed to make her an outcast. Having a father who was one of the world's top paranormal investigators had its perks. She'd seen and done more in her thirteen years than most people do in a lifetime. But the world was also full of skeptics, and Violet had learned that sometimes the less people knew about the family business, the better.

She checked herself in the visor mirror. A week ago she had dyed bright purple streaks into her jet black hair. It had seemed so cool at the time, and it definitely matched her striped purple shirt and black skirt. It would have been a great look if she had convinced her dad to bring her to London. Now it was a ticket to weird girl status.

Maybe I should start working on blending in, she thought. *Keep my head down and suck it up for six weeks.* She ran her fingers along a strand of purple poking out of her hair clip. Even with her head down she was going to stick out like a priest in a den of vampires.

She fondled the silver ankh that she wore around her neck, a gift from her mother. The ankh was an ancient symbol for eternal life: a cross on the bottom with a loop on top representing infinity. Mom had told her it would always keep her safe. But Violet knew it would take more than an Egyptian trinket to avoid the dangers of the world.

Her mother had been an anthropologist. She collected charms like the ankh from around the globe. Even if the charm didn't always make Violet feel safe, it did make her feel like somehow Mom was always around.

"Well there it is!" her father declared. A "Camp Coldwater" sign directed them down a dusty road. They passed under a metal archway displaying "COLDWATER" in sharp angular letters.

The dirt road wound through patches of pine trees and ended in a circular village of log cabins. Her father pulled up to a long building that appeared to be the main office. Three tan school buses lined the other side of the lot. Kids gathered outside them, shoving one another, screaming, and laughing.

"This is a summer camp, not a mental asylum, right?" Violet asked.

"You promised you'd stop complaining." Her father turned off the engine.

"Sorry, Daddy." She forced a smile. "At least you drove me here to check things out in person and didn't force me into a hot sweaty bus full of strange kids."

"Yes, I can be quite generous, can't I?" He opened his door and stretched outside.

"So generous," Violet muttered. "So generous that you're only forcing me to *live* with a bunch of strange kids for six weeks." She clutched the ankh around her neck. A little extra protection this summer would be a good thing.

She got out of the car and surveyed the grounds. The cabins themselves were not as dilapidated or rustic as she had feared. But she somehow doubted they were equipped with much in the way of modern convenience on the inside.

"I'm going to find a restroom, Violet. Why don't you take a look around and meet me back here in a few minutes?"

"Sure thing, Pops." As she watched him enter the office, she secretly hoped the bathroom would be squalid enough that he would refuse to leave her.

A boy screamed across the lot, "Leave me alone!"

頑

Violet turned her attention back to the crowd of rowdy kids by the busses. She cringed as two identical hulking blond thugs grabbed a scrawny boy by his ankles and dragged him facedown through the dirt. Onlookers erupted into laughter. The victimized boy squirmed free and stumbled to his feet. He had a short black crew cut, dark eyes, and a white polo that was now smeared with brown dust. Standing up, his face barely came to his tormentors' chests. He twisted his limbs uselessly as the two hulking blonds hoisted him into the air.

A third hulk stepped forward. They were triplets. The third boy lifted the little guy's feet and pulled his shoes off. *This is too painful to watch,* Violet thought. She took a deep breath and headed towards the disturbance.

Blond hulk three tied the boy's shoes together, spun them like a bola, and flung them into the treetops. A chorus of cheers resounded from the triplets' pack of pals. A clique of girls pointed and giggled. Violet wondered where all the adults were.

"Hey! Three Stooges!" Violet said. "Show's over. Let him go, and try to pick on people your own size going forward. Like, you know, each other." She glared at hulk three.

Hulk three sized her up. "Heh heh . . . what?" His brothers dropped the kid into the dirt, dopey grins plastered over their faces.

"Um . . . Leave boy alone." Violet gestured to the dirty shoeless kid, whose face was now beet red.

"What are you, the counselor?" Hulk three snickered. He wiped sweat from his rectangular forehead.

Violet nodded. "Yep. I am the junior counselor in charge of regulating jerk-like behavior on the grounds. So please, consider this a warning."

The three boys exchanged confused smiles. The lead triplet said, "All right, we'll leave him alone. Whatever. Happy Harry takes care of the shrimpiest kids anyway."

"Come again?" Violet asked.

The lead triplet got right in her face. Violet stood her ground, craning her neck as far back as she could to make eye contact. "Happy Harry," hulk three said. "He only takes the youngest, most innocent kids. So it pays to get a little bullying in on day one, punky. Nice hair by the way."

"Thanks." Violet smiled. "I'm glad you got all that bullying out of your system then. How about you leave this guy alone from now on?"

"I don't know. How about I pound your face until it's as purple as your little highlights there?"

"Well I know a refined gentleman like yourself wouldn't hit a lady, now would he?" Violet curtsied. A few kids nearby laughed.

Hulk three sneered.

"Don't hit a girl, Trent. Not worth it," one of his brothers said.

Trent scowled, then stomped his foot and balled up his fist suddenly at Violet, as if to make her flinch.

She held her ground. There was no way this overweight thug was going to deck her on the first day of camp. Maybe later in the week he might. After she'd had a chance to really put him in his place.

He turned back to the crowd and smiled. "All right. I guess your weird new friend just saved your butt, Chang."

"Hey campers!" a tall blond-bearded man shouted through a megaphone by the main office. "This is Head Counselor Gary making a very special announcement! I want everybody right here! Line up! Boys to the right, girls to the left! Everyone else can go home! Who's ready for fun, fun, fun!"

The crowd of kids meandered towards the office.

"I said, who's ready for FUN!" Head Counselor Gary screamed.

A few insincere cheers erupted.

"That's more like it!"

As the crowd dispersed, Violet approached the dusty kid on the ground. *Why couldn't this counselor have come five minutes ago?* she wondered. *If he had intervened, it might not have been as embarrassing for the poor guy.* She offered the boy her hand.

He took it. She hoisted him onto his dirty socks and introduced herself, "Violet Black. Sorry if I overstepped myself there."

"No, it's okay. I'm Hector. Hector Chang. Those guys are the worst. Every summer, I swear to God! They're just the worst!" He sounded on the verge of tears.

"Why don't you just tell the counselors?"

"No, no, no! Any time I tell on them, it gets worse. The things they do to me, I swear. God, I hate them! I wish they would all just die!" he screamed.

"Hey, easy. They're jerks, but let's not get carried away." Violet dusted off Hector's shirt.

He shooed her away. "Sorry, sorry. Sorry! Just forget about me. Don't bother next time; it'll just make them pick on you too. God, I hate them!"

Violet laughed. "Don't worry about me, Hector. I'm pretty much un-pick-on-able. People tend not to like me either, but I just try not to let it bother me."

"Where did they throw my shoes? Where are my shoes! Argh! I hate those guys!" Hector's face burned red. His arms shook as he searched.

"It's okay, buddy. They just tossed them over there." Violet pointed out the gray and orange gym shoes dangling over a low hanging branch. "Not even that high."

Hector scrambled over to the tree and jumped up and down desperately. He whacked the soles of his shoes, but he couldn't quite free them. Violet sighed. Hector actually *was* too short to get them down, but she was pretty sure she could do it.

After a few more failed attempts on Hector's part, Violet jumped up and grabbed the shoes. "Here you go."

Hector's face turned a darker shade of crimson.

"I think you freed up the laces when you were hitting the bottoms," she offered.

"Yeah, shut up," Hector said wearily. He got to work on Trent's knot. "Thanks."

"Don't mention it." Violet thought back to what Trent had said before they were interrupted. "So who the heck is Happy Harry anyway?"

"Oh, it's this stupid ghost story the campers tell."

"Huh." Violet helped Hector to his feet once he'd freed his laces and gotten his shoes back on. "You know, I've never heard that one."

"You will," Hector said. They made their way towards the office. "You'll probably know the whole dumb thing by heart soon enough."

2

Violet walked her dad back to his car after the first hour of orientation had gone to his satisfaction. She knew he was on a tight schedule, driving to and from Camp Coldwater in one day, so she wanted to make this a quick, painless goodbye.

He hugged her tight. "You know, they allow parents to stay through the orientation, darling."

Violet opened the driver's side door and ushered him inside. "I'll be fine, Dad. Really. You need to get organized and catch a plane tomorrow."

"You're sure you're all right?"

She rolled her eyes. "I'm fine! I made a friend already."

"Just an hour ago you were begging me not to leave you." He buckled his seatbelt and sized her up. "Makes me think you're up to something."

She shrugged. "I am planning a hostile takeover. I hope to avoid unnecessary bloodshed."

He laughed. "I have no doubt you'll be running this place by the time I'm back."

Violet leaned through the open window and kissed his cheek. "Get lost, old man."

Her father gave a final wave as he pulled away. His car disappeared in a cloud of dirt behind the pine trees.

"All right campers! Listen up!" came another enthusiastic announcement from Head Counselor Gary's megaphone. "It's

11

super important that *all* campers report to the north courtyard for cabin assignment! Once again, moms and dads are welcome to hang out until tonight's barbeque. But we need all campers! On the north courtyard! Right now! Five minutes ago! Let's get a move on!" Gary snorted before turning off his megaphone.

Violet inhaled deeply and clutched her mom's ankh. Cabin assignments could make or break the summer. She rounded the north side of the office. A huge crowd of kids had gathered on the brick patio. Violet guessed there had to be at least seventy campers.

Gary stood atop a stone platform backed by ten college-aged counselors. Violet scanned the crowd for Hector, but gave up after a few minutes. Either he was too short to be found, or perhaps, he had made a break for it.

"Remember campers! We did our best to accommodate your special roomie requests, but it's four to a cabin, so you might not always be able to bunk with your buddies!" Gary's smile was almost too big for his face. "But the best part is: you might make some *new* buddies!"

The crowd collectively groaned. One boy shouted, "I want to be *your* buddy, Gary!"

"Okay, sounds good!" Gary replied. "When you hear your name, come on up! After that, my junior counselors will take you to check out your rustic digs for a bunkmate meet-n-greet!" Violet did not like the sound of rustic digs.

"Cabin number 1!" Gary held a finger in the air to indicate "one." His list of names crinkled. He read off a list of boys. Violet tried her best to match names and faces as they made their way to the stage. She recognized a few from the scene by the school buses earlier.

"Cabin 6!" He glanced down at his list. "Trent Tucker! Brent Tucker! Brant Tucker!"

Violet stifled laughter as the three hulking blond triplets from before made their way up. *Trent, Brent, and Brant?* Each name sounded like a punch in the face. She wondered if their parents had purposefully named them to be thugs.

"Aaaaand . . ." Gary scanned his list again for the fourth name. "Hector Chang! Come on up, Hector!"

A deep pit burrowed into Violet's stomach. Hector emerged from the crowd, pale as a dead man. The Tucker triplets sported goblin grins as a pale blond counselor led them off the stage towards the cabins. She hoped Hector would be in one piece the next time she saw him. *If things get bad enough, the Tucker Triplets will be kicked out of camp,* she assured herself. *Or at least Hector could be moved to another room. How unreasonable could Camp Coldwater be?*

Soon Gary was reading off the girl's names. "Cabin 28!" Gary shouted. "Becky Montana!"

A bubbly blond danced her way up to the stage. When Becky reached the platform, she tossed her hair as if she was about to accept an Academy Award. Her pink halter top spelled "platinum blonde" in glittering silver.

"Doesn't she know all the boys are gone?" Violet heard another girl mutter nearby. "Who is she showing off for?"

"Ronny St. Claire!" Gary called out.

A skinny girl with freckles and frizzy red hair screamed with delight and raced up to the stage. Ronny and Becky clutched hands and screeched together like old friends who hadn't seen one another in decades. *Looks like Becky has a sidekick,* Violet thought.

"Violet Black!" Gary shouted.

"Son of a . . ." Violet sighed and made her way through the thinning crowd, trying to appear friendly. *Maybe rooming with Miss America and her bubbly friend won't be that bad,* she hoped. *If not, maybe Hector can switch with me.*

"Kelly Powers!" Gary said as Violet climbed on stage. A tall lean African American girl in a blue and yellow basketball jersey made her way up. Kelly's hair was tied in a neat black bun behind her head. Her soft brown eyes contrasted a stern expression. Violet smiled and waved. Kelly nodded politely, but did not return a smile.

Becky and Ronny, on the other hand, had yet to acknowledge either of them. They were chattering amongst themselves at what was possibly the speed of light.

A short, chubby brunette with a clip board motioned for them to follow, and the four girls headed out. Ronny and Becky's chattering grew louder and faster as they crossed the clearing towards the cabins.

Ronny's voice inflected upwards at the end of every sentence. "OMG! I swear to God! I knew! I just knew we would room together! I swear, I had like a feeling!"

"Oh for sure!" Becky walked with her head tilted up. She never made eye contact with Ronny who seemed to hang on her every word. "I knew they would definitely put us together because, like, the counselors here really like me. I mean I've been coming up here for like five years. It's cool that we're rooming together though. You know?"

The junior counselor opened the door to a modest log cabin. "Cabin 28!" There were two sets of bunk beds and two bureaus with four drawers each. A door on the left led to a small bathroom. "You each get a bed, and . . ." the counselor knocked on one of the wooden bureaus, "two of these drawers. You share. You respect each other. You respect the girls next door. You respect the camp's property. Got it?"

The four girls nodded.

The counselor glared, eyes thick with black liner. Her dark blue lips drawn tight. "Schedules are posted at the office. Your schedule corresponds to your cabin number. You look for cabin 28. You follow that schedule. Questions?"

Silence.

"Good. Means I don't have to talk as much." She wiped her nose on the back of her wrist, smearing her lipstick a little. "You got an hour of free time. Then everybody comes to the BBQ tonight at six."

The counselor started to walk away. Violet called out, "Um, do you have a name?"

The counselor turned and sneered. "I'm not your personal caretaker, missy. The counselor you report to varies from day to day. From one activity to the next. Check your schedule."

"Oh," Violet said. "Well I just wanted to say hello."

"Hi!" The woman gave a curt salute with her free hand. "I'm Sassy."

"Charmed." Violet forced a smile.

Without another word, Sassy headed back to the courtyard to attend another batch of girls.

"Well." Violet turned to her new roommates. "That was brief and to the point. Do you think Sassy was actually her name or just an ill-fitted description of her personality?"

Kelly smiled.

"Who cares!" Becky tossed her pink duffel bag on the nearest top bunk. "I call dibs on this bed, unless the other one is comfier. Then I call dibs on *that* one."

Ronny stared from one side of the room to the other. "Should I take the other top bunk? Or should I take the bottom bunk? What's the easiest way to talk to each other at night?"

Violet tried to come up with something constructive to say in response to either girl, then gave up and turned to Kelly. "Hi, I'm Violet."

Kelly provided a firm handshake. "Kelly Powers."

"How long do you guys take to get ready in the morning? Because I need at least an hour and forty minutes," Becky said as she inspected the bathroom.

Again, Violet wasn't quite sure how to respond. "Not exactly the bunkmate meet-n-greet I was expecting," she finally said.

Ronny crinkled her nose. "The what-what?"

"That's what Gary called the--" Violet shook her head. "I mean I kind of thought the counselors would make us play 'the name game' or something before they just cut us loose to form little societies like this."

Ronny and Becky ignored her. Ronny picked up a plunger off the bathroom floor. "What's this?"

Violet took a deep breath and turned to Kelly. "I think I need some air. Care to join me?"

Kelly shrugged and nodded. They left their bags on top of the nearest dresser and wandered outside as Ronny squealed with disgust about something she had found in the shower.

Outside, a cool breeze blew from across Lake Coldwater. Kelly seemed like the strong silent type, but if Violet was going to survive rooming with Princess Peroxide and her handmaid this summer, she was going to need some kind of ally.

"So . . . they seem . . . nice," Violet offered.

"They're not." Kelly smiled.

Violet relaxed. "Have you been coming here long? Do you go to school with any of these kids?"

"Some of them," Kelly said. "Becky and Ronny since first grade. Where you from?"

"Kinda all over," Violet said. "My dad moves a lot. He's a professor. He might take a job in Northern Wisconsin at the end of the summer, so I think he thought Camp Coldwater would be a convenient place to find me in August."

"You play any sports?" Kelly asked.

"Is chess a sport?"

"No."

"Then no. But I have great respect for speed skaters."

"Well, I like to win, and Becky and Ronny are hopeless. So since they always do teams by cabin, you might be my only hope. Are you trainable?"

Violet laughed nervously. "I promise that I will *try* to try at sports this summer if you promise that you are a sane person to live with."

"Deal." Kelly offered her hand, and they shook.

The clearing in front of their cabin led to a dark patch of trees that lined the lake. Sassy led another group of four girls past them, and Violet gave a friendly wave. Sassy shot her a dirty look and continued on.

3

Fortunately, campers were not forced to sit with their roommates at the barbeque. Becky and Ronny made a beeline for some much more popular girls once they arrived back at the courtyard. Picnic tables, benches, and fire pits surrounded the lakefront. As night darkened, counselors lit bright bonfires. The reflections sparkled across the surface of the water. Violet had to admit the view was breathtaking, even if her hotdog tasted like shoe leather.

Violet and Kelly sat at the end of a long table. They had managed to get each other up to speed on some basic icebreaker info. Kelly was the oldest girl in a family of five. She had four little brothers, and she loved running, basketball, and karate. Her mother was a teacher, and her father was a doctor.

Violet tried her best to be honest, but couldn't help modifying the details of her own life here and there. She said her father was a professor of English rather than parapsychology. She also said her mother had died in an auto accident. Sudden and random, that at least was true.

"So you don't play any sports at all?" Kelly asked for the third time.

Violet shook her head.

"You don't watch TV?"

Violet rolled her eyes and shook her head.

"And you're not into fashion?"

Violet shrugged. "I kind of have my own style."

Kelly smiled. "I can see that. I wouldn't dye my hair purple, but you pull it off."

"Thanks."

"So what do you do for fun then? What do you do with your friends?"

"Well my family travels a lot. I hang around with a lot of adults. I read. I assist my dad at . . . literature conferences and . . . you know, different things."

"You like movies?"

"Sure, I just usually like the book better."

"You like computers?"

"I try to like them, but they hate me."

Kelly laughed. "Same here."

Violet felt good about Kelly. At least she had one solid roommate, even if they didn't seem to have much in common. "So what exactly do we do all day here? Play sports, hike, and eat leather hotdogs?" Violet dumped the remainder of her half-eaten dog onto her plate and continued to eat the bun.

"They do some woodshop, arts and crafts; there's a drama club. It's like school with just activities and no class. First few weeks everybody does a little of everything. Later, they let you sign up for more of what you like."

Violet nodded. "I might survive this."

"You will." Kelly pointed to Violet's half eaten hotdog. "You done with that?"

"You *want* it?"

Kelly made a face. "No! I was just going to toss it and check the schedule for tomorrow." Kelly stood and stacked their plates. "Wanna come?"

Violet spotted Hector wandering alone through the tables.

"Actually, I made a buddy earlier, and I have to check on him. I'll catch up with you though."

"Cool." Kelly took off.

Violet waved her arms in the air until Hector finally spotted her. He gestured to himself and mouthed, "Me?"

"Yes you! Get over here!" Violet beckoned him.

Hector rushed over. "Hi! I can't believe you even remember me!"

"I can't believe those Tucker Triplets haven't eaten you alive yet." Violet gestured for him to sit down. "How you holding up?"

He slumped. "I can't believe it! Can you believe it? The whole summer! The whole summer with those jerks! I hate my parents! I hate those guys. Oh my God! I can't believe it!" Hector's plate overflowed with two hotdogs, a burger, and a heaping pile of potato chips. Once his rant concluded, he proceeded to stuff his face.

"Let me guess, Hector. You're one of those people who eats and eats and never gains a pound?"

"Mm hummgry!" Hector muffled through his mouthful.

"I can see that." Violet smiled. "Well don't feel too bad. I got a couple of iffy roommates myself. It's going to be a long summer, so we should start brainstorming about how we're going to make it to the end."

Hector swallowed. "Do you think they'll let me switch rooms? You know what Brent and Brant did to me after the counselor left us alone? They put their fingers in their mouths and stuck them in my ears!"

"Ew!" Violet cringed. "Wet Willy, huh?"

"No, Brent and Brant. Trent held me down."

"No, it's called a Wet Willy. When you stick your finger--" Violet shook her head. "Never mind. We should talk to Gary about changing your room."

Hector chomped his burger as he talked, "It jmst mmkes it wormse!"

"Maybe try chewing with your mouth closed, buddy?"

Hector ingested a handful of crumbling chips. "Sorry, hmgry."

Hector was short, weak, a motor mouth, and kinda gross to top it off. Violet had a feeling he would be getting himself into all kinds of trouble, all summer long. She was about to tactfully broach the topic of table manners when suddenly Head Counselor Gary appeared and put his arms around each of their shoulders. "Hey, you two! Having fun?"

"Sure," Violet said.

Hector muffled something incomprehensible through his crunching chips.

"Super! Tell you what! We're about to tell a *scary* story around the fire. How'd you guys like to come on over to my circle? All the kids know that *Scary* Gary tells the best campfire stories!"

Hector swallowed and made an annoyed face. "Not Happy Harry."

Gary glared but kept his upbeat tone, "It might not be Happy Harry. It might be a different story. You'll have to join the circle," he tapped his ears, "and listen up to find out!" Gary wandered over to the next table.

Violet stifled laughter. "That guy is too peppy for words."

"Every year people tell that dumb story. I wish Happy Harry was my roommate instead of those stupid Tucker jerks!"

"Hey! Everybody gather round a fire! It's story time!" Gary called out. Next to each bonfire, a counselor waved a flashlight in the air. "Bring your food! Gather round! Time for *fun*!"

"I kind of want to hear the story," Violet said. "Come on."

"It's stupid," Hector said. "It's stupid, and it's scary."

"I don't scare easy." Violet stood. "Come on, you can bring your pile of food."

Hector shook his head. "No thanks."

"Suit yourself. Keep your chin up."

Hector mumbled something through his hotdog.

Violet approached Gary's campfire. She found a vacant spot at the edge of a log bench. Gary held his flashlight beneath his chin, casting an eerie glow upon his face.

"I'm glad everyone is here around this fire where it's safe."

Gary's voice dropped several octaves. Violet squinted in the firelight to makes sure it was still him. "Tonight's story is important because, well , , . believing it could mean the difference between life and death." The circle grew quiet and still. Gary surveyed the crowd.

Gary should talk this way all the time, Violet thought. His phony scary voice was much more bearable than his phony enthusiastic voice.

"Some of you may have heard this story before, in years gone by. But it's important to hear it again," Gary continued. "I want to make absolutely sure that you all know what you're dealing with out there." He aimed his flashlight into the trees.

"There once was a family who lived in these woods. The father's name was Harry. Harry was a good man. He worked hard. He chopped and sold lumber, cherished his children, and loved his wife truly and deeply.

"The life the family lived was simple, but they were all extraordinarily happy." Gary paced around the fire. "One day, Harry returned home to find that his beloved wife had passed away. Some say she had a weak heart, others that she took ill.

Regardless, her death shocked the family. Harry's wonderful world turned upside down.

"He fell into deep . . . dark . . . despair. He could barely bring himself to eat, sleep, work, or provide for his children. He wandered the forest with his trusty hickory stemmed ax, trying to force himself to chop trees and put food on his family's table. But he was a shell of his former self. He would have given anything to be happy again. Anything at all." Light and shadow danced up Gary's face.

"One evening, the Devil appeared to Harry on his way home. He offered a deal. If Harry agreed to his favors, the Devil, in exchange, would make him happier. Happier than he had ever been before. For the sake of his family, Harry was desperate to gain the strength to move past his wife's death. So he agreed without realizing how dark and terrible the Devil's deeds would be.

"Once every full moon, the Devil asked Harry to kill one of his neighbors. He slaughtered them with his trusty ax, one by one, then dragged them down the forest path and presented them to his master. In exchange, the Devil held up his end of the bargain. He made Harry happier.

"At first Harry wanted to fight the arrangement, but with each murder, he experienced incredible euphoria. Joy far beyond the love he felt for his wife and children. It was a dark, intoxicating happiness. Like a drug. And every time Harry killed . . . he wanted more.

"Soon Harry had killed so many that he was no longer the same man. Eventually, he stopped caring even for his family." A log crumbled on the bonfire, spitting sparks into the darkness.

"They too fell prey to his terrible ax. They say he grinned ear to ear as he chopped them up . . . and offered them to his dark lord."

A chill breeze crept over the shore. The embers of the bonfire crackled up behind Gary's shadowy face.

"Nobody quite knows what became of Happy Harry, but many believe he still wanders these woods, whistling a happy tune. His trusty hickory ax slung over his shoulder. Waiting for the next innocent young thing to cross his path. They say that Harry prefers children because he derives such intense pleasure from slaying the pure and innocent."

The entire circle fell dead quiet. "So as you walk back to your cabins tonight, make sure you stay on the grounds. Never wander into the woods after sunset. And if you hear a happy little tune echoing through the trees: be afraid. That's Happy Harry. Walking along. Waiting for campers to stray too far into his woods."

Gary whistled a happy tune that Violet recognized as the march from the Russian symphony "Peter and the Wolf." He circled the fire towards Violet as he whistled. He got closer. Closer.

Suddenly, he jumped at a different camper nearby and shouted. The boy shrieked in horror, and the entire circle erupted into laughter.

Gary patted the boy's shoulder. His super excited counselor voice returned, "Hope I didn't scare you too much, champ! It's just a story!" He held the flashlight under his face again. "Or *is* it!" Then he laughed. "Man we're having *fun* tonight, huh guys and gals?"

Violet stepped away from the circle. She was impressed by Gary's storytelling, although unnerved by the way he dropped in and out of his different personas. She returned to her picnic table to find Kelly looking over a piece of paper. Hector had split.

"Hey," Violet said. "That Happy Harry story was actually kind of creepy."

Kelly nodded, wide-eyed. "I heard the end of Sassy's version. The counselors usually clean it up a little when they tell it to kids. They're supposed leave out the parts about killing his family. Parents are gonna complain."

"Hey, we're big kids. We can take it." Violet shrugged. "I thought it was neat, but you know I'm into . . . literature."

Kelly handed her the piece of paper. "Tomorrow's schedule."

Violet unfolded a grid of cabin numbers and activities.

"Canoeing, first thing in the morning. Totally not hard, two to a boat, so we won't have to work with Becky and Ronny."

"I can live with that." Violet scanned the other activities: a two-hour hike, baseball, archery, and a movie on self-esteem. Not her ideal week, but at least she was making friends.

By 9:30, most of the campers were making their way back to the cabins. Gary made an announcement that everyone had to be indoors by 10:00, lights out by 11:00. Violet turned to Kelly. "If we hurry back, maybe we'll be exhausted enough to fall asleep before Becky and Ronny get back."

Kelly agreed, and they returned to cabin 28. As Kelly got ready for bed, Violet leaned against the window. A dark crescent lined the moon, and a sea of stars glimmered. "Hey, I'm going outside to look for constellations," Violet called out.

"Cool!" Kelly shouted from the bathroom. "I'll join you in a sec!"

Violet wandered outside and craned her neck up. She found the big dipper and the North Star. "Pretty amazing," she whispered to herself. It wasn't too often she got to gaze at the stars in the middle of nowhere. All things considered, camp could be worse.

A blood curdling scream echoed in the night. Violet glanced down and spotted a frantic shadow racing from the woods towards the cabins: a camper. The child tripped and scrambled back to his feet, still shouting in terror. Violet raced out to meet him.

Hector collided with her and knocked her to the ground. His scream grated against her ears. Tears streamed down his face.

"Run!" he shouted.

Violet got back to her feet. She held his shoulders and tried to steady him. "Hey, calm down. It's okay."

"It's *not* okay!" He wrestled out of her arms and turned every which way as if he expected someone behind him. Then he grabbed Violet's arms. "I saw him! I saw Happy Harry! And he tried to kill me!"

4

Head Counselor Gary, two of his junior counselors, and a small crowd of snickering kids had gathered around Hector and Violet. Hector gasped out heavy breaths. His hands shook.

"Hey now, champ!" Gary patted Hector's back. "You're okay. You just got spooked out there in the dark!"

"I *know* what I saw!" Hector shoved Gary's hand away; his eyes remained fixed on the trees. "It was a tall man with an ax and a torn up coat. He had a leathery face--"

"You imagined it." Gary shook his head.

"I *didn't!*" Hector said.

Laughter erupted from the crowd of kids. Junior Counselor Sassy raised a fist at them. "Shaddup!"

"You know," Violet said, "he seems serious. Maybe someone really *did* jump out at him." She lowered her voice so that only Gary and Hector could hear. "Some other kids were picking on us earlier. I think maybe one of them was playing a prank."

Hector shook his head.

"Well, we'll keep our eyes out for anything spooky," Gary said. "You guys are safe here. There's nothing to be afraid of." He turned to the crowd of kids. "Everyone back to your cabins. Get ready for bed. Lights out at 11:00! Big day tomorrow! Big *fun* day!"

"You heard the man," Sassy snapped. "Get!"

The other kids meandered back towards the cabins. The Tucker Triplets made up the rear, each sporting an identically dirty grin. "See you at home, Chang!"

Gary nodded to Sassy and the other counselors. "Follow those kids. Make sure they go straight back to their cabins." He turned back to Violet and Hector. "And you two, don't worry about a thing. I'll check the woods. I'll make sure we don't have any pranksters spoiling our summer fun. Sound good?"

"Sounds good." Violet forced a smile.

"Super!"

"It wasn't a prank!" Hector insisted.

"Sure it was!" Gary continued off in the direction of the bonfires. Violet couldn't help but wonder why he wasn't headed towards the trees where Hector had supposedly been attacked. Wouldn't that be the best place to get to the bottom of the whole thing?

"Violet!" Hector grabbed her arm. "I'm *not* joking! It was him."

"Hey, I believe you saw something," she said. "But let's try to figure out what, okay?"

"It was Happy . . . Harry!"

"Look Hec, I like you pal, but it seems like you have more than your fair share of tormentors here. One of the boring truths of the world is that the simplest explanation is almost always correct. It was probably one of those lug heads you're rooming with dressed up in a scary costume, just to mess with you. Don't give them the satisfaction."

"The Tucker Triplets are short and fat," Hector said. "This guy was tall and thin."

"It was dark, though. Did the guy wear a mask?"

"I think. His face was like a fleshy . . . stitched together sort of--"

"Hector, ghosts don't wear masks. People dressed up like ghosts do."

"His eyes glowed. Like fire! He had eight eyes, all glowing. They lit up the forest!" Hector glanced back. "We have to get back inside; he's out there!"

"It doesn't look like anyone's out there now."

"He came after me. With an *ax*!"

"I believe you, okay?" Violet placed her hand on his shoulder. "I believe you saw a man with an ax. But you have to keep your cool. He probably only had an ax because he wanted you to scream and run."

"He swiped it! Right at my head!" Hector made a horizontal chopping motion at Violet's face. "He tried to *kill* me! Why won't anyone believe me?"

Violet bit her lip. She'd seen her fair share of strange and dangerous things. But she'd seen even more false alarms. "I do believe you, Hector. Until I find proof that there's *not* an ax-wielding lunatic in the woods, I will proceed as if there is one. Fair enough?"

Hector sighed. "Okay." He glared at the shadowy pine trees.

"What were you doing walking around in the woods alone, anyway?" Violet asked.

"I figured if I waited until the Tuckers were asleep, they wouldn't do annoying things to me when I got back to the cabin. So I took a walk."

"You're sure it wasn't just one of those jerks, dressed up?"

"I wish. If it was one of them, I could get them in trouble and send them home and . . . and . . . and then that thing I saw wouldn't be *real!*"

Hector sounded on the verge of tears again. Whatever he saw, Violet decided, *he* believed it was real. That was good enough for her. "Why don't I take you back? You'll feel safer indoors."

Hector continued to stare. "I'm afraid."

"Afraid to go to your cabin?"

"Afraid that the second I turn my back on those trees, he's going to come after me."

Crickets chirped in the distance.

"Well," Violet suggested, "if the story is true, then Happy Harry won't come after you unless you're in the woods, right?"

"That's comforting." Hector took a deep breath.

Violet tugged his arm. "Come on." She walked him back in silence. The whole way he continued to sneak glances over his shoulder. When they arrived, his cabin was pitch black. The Tuckers weren't back yet. More evidence that they could be out in the forest laughing it up. She considered a quick search of the cabin to see if she could find incriminating evidence, but the Tuckers could be back any minute. The last thing she wanted was to cause more grief for Hector.

Inside, Hector rummaged through his bag. "I dropped my light in the woods, but I have another one." He found a black flashlight. "Here." He gave it to Violet.

"Hector, I think I can find my way. It's a pretty well-lit area."

"Just take it. Be careful." He could barely make eye contact as she accepted the flashlight. "I'm such a dork," he said.

"No you're not."

"Yes I am. I totally am! You walked me home, and I should walk *you* home and make sure you're safe and everything."

Violet tried not to laugh. "That's sweet, Hector. I accept your flashlight of protection. Just get some sleep, and I'll see you tomorrow, okay?"

"Thanks. Be careful."

Violet was halfway back to her cabin when she decided to take a detour. She crossed the open field to the trees where Hector had been "attacked." His flashlight was coming in handy after all.

She performed a slow, methodical sweep of the area with the beam of light: trees, dirt, leaves, weeds. Everything seemed normal. She entered the woods and found a walking path. Moonlight streamed through the canopy. A distant chorus of frogs accompanied the crickets. Far to her left, bonfires flickered along with the muffled voices of counselors. She could understand how almost *anything* that moved under these dark conditions could set off a touchy kid like Hector.

Her eye caught a thin ray of light in the weeds: Hector's other flashlight. It was smaller than the one he had given Violet, something he would have carried in his pocket. She guided her light across a dusty path in the trees that led towards the bonfires. Hector had gotten bored with the barbeque, taken out his pocket flashlight, and made his way down this path to kill time before the Tuckers fell asleep. Then he got to this point and saw what, exactly?

Violet picked up the second flashlight. Hector was prepared. He had packed two flashlights of two different sizes. Violet hadn't even thought to bring one. She stepped onto the dirt path and aimed her beams in both directions. No people in sight, but streaks in the sandy path suggested a disturbance.

She moved to the side of the pathway and ran her lights along the ground. Gym shoe prints, about Hector's size, then a big smear where he stopped in his tracks and scrambled to the trees.

She scanned the path in the other direction and found two bold boot prints, large men's boots. She couldn't seem to find which direction they had come from, but whoever jumped out at Hector had probably been hiding in the trees, so that made sense. Someone had definitely startled him.

She ran her flashlight beams up and down the nearby trees. Finally, her lights landed upon something unusual: a deep, horizontal notch in the trunk of an oak tree. It appeared to be fresh, and it came up to Violet's neck . . . or Hector's skull.

She took a closer look, illuminating dark black lines around the edges of the notch. The bark appeared to have been burned.

"Violet!"

Violet twisted in surprise.

Kelly shielded her eyes from the flashlight beams. "Ah! Bright!"

"Sorry." She lowered the beams and offered a flashlight to Kelly. "That kid Hector says he got attacked out here, and I wanted to see for myself."

Kelly laughed. "Hector Chang? It was probably just some jerk picking on him."

Violet took one last look at the notch in the tree. "Yeah, that's what I thought . . ."

"Come on." Kelly patted her back. "It's almost lights out, and we don't want to get in trouble."

"Right." Violet followed Kelly back towards the cabin. "We definitely don't want any of that."

5

The next morning, Becky and Ronny owned the bathroom. After discovering that breakfast would only last another hour, Violet and Kelly freshened up as best they could and headed out.

At the dining hall, Violet poked at a runny yellow substance with her plastic fork. She had thought it was Jell-O, but now she wondered if it was supposed to be scrambled eggs.

"Yeah, I wouldn't eat that," Kelly said. "Stick with the basics." She gestured to her tray. "Apple, individually boxed cereal, OJ in a bottle. Stuff not even Camp Coldwater can screw up. Here." She handed Violet her apple. "I'll get another one on the way out."

"Thanks." Violet inspected it for wormholes then took a big juicy bite. "So this Happy Harry story: how long have they been telling it here?"

"You're still thinking about last night?" Kelly added milk to her cereal. "I don't know. Before my time. You shouldn't stress out about Hector Chang. He's kind of deranged."

"I think sometimes kids use words like deranged too loosely," Violet suggested. "You mean he's weird, right?"

She nodded. "Okay, he's weird. I mean I feel bad for him and all . . ."

"Because he gets picked on?"

"Well yeah, but not just that. Every summer his parents ditch him here at camp, and he hates it. Last year, he actually broke his arm." Kelly lowered her voice, "He was *begging* to go home. It was sad."

"Wait? He broke his arm, and he couldn't go home? His parents wouldn't come get him?"

"They couldn't. Most of his family is overseas, I guess. The Philippines, I think. So in the summer they leave him here for six weeks and come back for him. I guess just because it's easier."

Violet's dad was probably departing for London at that very moment. Sounded like she and Hector had something in common. "Yeah, that's rough. Who broke Hector's arm last year?"

"I didn't say a person broke his arm. The kid's a klutz. He tripped and fell." She finished up her last spoonful of cereal. "I want to get a jog in before canoeing starts. You in?"

"I'm more of a leisurely stroll kind of person," Violet said. "Maybe we can walk, and I'll think about whether or not I might want to go faster next time."

Kelly laughed as she cleared her place. "All right. Let's take a walk outside, and I'll show you the path." Kelly grabbed an apple on the way out. They exited the back door and headed towards the lake. Violet stopped when she heard a loud clunking sound.

"What?" Kelly gave her a funny look.

Clunk! There it was again. "That noise." Violet wandered around the outside of the dining hall. Kelly followed.

"What noise?"

Clunk! As Violet rounded the corner, she saw Gary about twenty yards away. He stood before a tree stump with a log standing upright. He hoisted his arms and swung an ax downward. *Clunk!* He expertly split the lumber in two. Violet watched him set up another piece of wood and chop again. *Clunk!* "Gary swings a mean ax," Violet observed.

"Oh yeah, he's a real mountain man." Kelly giggled. "Who cares? Let's go!" She started jogging in place. "I'll race you!"

Violet watched Gary clunk one last piece of wood, then she took Kelly by the arm and wandered back in the direction of the lake. "Kelly, how long has Gary been the super happy fun-loving head counselor at Camp Coldwater. Was he always here?"

"He's new. At least he wasn't head counselor last summer."

"*Very* interesting. He's tall, and he's thin, and he swings a mean ax . . . and he's new," Violet thought aloud.

"So?"

"Just trying to stay up to speed as the new girl," Violet said. Gary also hadn't bothered to investigate the scene where his camper had been attacked. And he seemed to really get into that scary story.

Violet spotted a familiar short, dark-haired kid shuffling along the shore with his head down. "Hey Kel, I'm gonna take a rain check on our walk-jog."

Kelly noticed Hector. "You're a regular Good Samaritan, Violet Black. That boy's going to be in love with you if you keep hanging out with him."

"Well then he'll have good taste. I'll meet you at the dock. Canoes. 9:00. You teach; I'll try not to totally and completely stink."

"Deal. Later!" Kelly jogged down the same path where Hector had his encounter. Violet hoped that if there was a Happy Harry, he was nocturnal.

She found Hector hurling flat stones into the water. He couldn't seem to get them to skip. Violet picked one off the ground. "You've gotta give it some spin. Watch." She flung her rock, and it skidded across the murky water six times.

"You're good at everything, and I'm good at nothing," Hector muttered.

"Yeesh, I made a rock skip. They're not going to throw me a parade or anything." She gestured for Hector to walk with her and led him back towards the dining hall. "You eat breakfast?"

"I don't want to go in there; everyone will make fun of me."

"You want me to get you something?"

"Why are you being so nice to me?"

"Because . . ." Violet paused. She didn't want to say it was because she felt bad for him. "Because I don't really fit in here either, Hector. And I think the summer will be a lot more fun if we can hang out and not fit in at the same time."

Hector smiled. "I definitely don't fit in at all. Everyone hates me."

"I think you might be exaggerating a bit there, buddy." Violet steered the direction of their walk away from the main entrance and circled the building. "So are you thinking a little more clearly this morning about . . . stuff?"

"You don't believe me. It's no big deal. Nobody believes me. Everyone thinks I'm crazy now. The Tuckers made fun of me for crying. Half those kids saw me look stupid." He shook his head. "But if they saw what I saw . . ."

"I believe you, Hector." Violet looked him right in the eyes. "I really do. I just want to help you figure out what you saw."

Violet listened carefully. She no longer heard the clunking of Gary's ax. "For instance," she lowered her voice. "If you saw the ax that the guy had last night, would you recognize it?"

Hector's eyes widened. "Yes! Definitely! Oh my God, it was so weird!"

They rounded the corner. Gary was gone, but his ax remained propped against the tree stump. Violet approached and pointed. "Is that it?" The ax sported a polished wood handle with a flat charcoal-colored blade and red tip.

Hector examined it with a dull expression.

"Well?" Violet asked. "Sort of looked like this? Similar? I know it was dark."

"It wasn't dark!" Hector shook his head. "His eyes, they--"

"Glowed like hellfire, right. Sorry. But the ax--"

"Hey!" Gary rounded a cabin across the clearing. "Don't touch that!" he shouted. Once he approached, his tone changed. "We don't want to have an *ax*-ident, do we?" He smiled and ushered them away.

"Sorry, Gary! We were just looking. I saw you chopping up all that firewood and wanted to show Hector where our bonfires come from. So cool, right Hec?" Her forced enthusiasm rivaled Gary's.

Hector just stared at her. "Why are you talking like that?"

"Well okay," Gary said. "But I'll bet you guys have activities starting soon. Get some breakfast in you! Breakfast is the lumber for the *bonfire* of a fun day!"

"I never thought of it that way!" Violet grabbed Hector by the arm. "Come on, Hector; let's fuel up!" She dragged him back towards the front of the building, away from the potential ax murderer.

She pulled Hector aside and lowered her voice. "Happy Harry was about Gary's height right? Six foot one? Six foot two?"

"Yeah."

"And who was the first person on the scene after you ran out of the woods? After I found you?"

"Gary."

"Right, Gary. And who do I find this morning slicing up lumber with an ax?"

"Gary," Hector said. "But--"

"Now I'm not saying anything one way or the other here." Violet paced. "But remember what I said about the most reasonable explanations usually being the right ones?"

"Yeah, but--"

"And Gary was so quick to dismiss your story. He saw how hysterical you were, and he didn't even take you back to your cabin. Or calm you down. What kind of head counselor--"

"Violet!" Hector shouted.

"What?"

"That ax was *not* Happy Harry's ax."

"It wasn't?"

"Not even close." Hector shook his head. "Happy Harry's ax," he ran his hands through the air along an imaginary weapon, "had this long, gnarled handle. It was all twisted. The blade was *huge*! It came out to this hooked C shape. And it . . . this is hard to explain, but it gave off heat. Like he'd just held it in a fire or something. It was out of this world." Hector shook his head. "I don't know how else to explain it."

Violet nodded. She'd seen this look on people's faces before. Hector really believed what he was saying, and she was starting to think he really did see something far weirder than Gary in a costume. "Okay," she said. "I believe you."

"You do?"

"Yep."

Hector shook his head. "But why? I wouldn't believe me. It's crazy."

"Can you keep a secret?"

"Who would I tell? Everyone hates me."

"Well I don't hate you, Hector. In fact, I think I'd like to do you a favor."

"What?"

"I'm going to take your case."

"My case?"

Violet nodded. "I'm kind of a ghost hunter."

Hector's eyes widened.

"What? You thought you were the only weird kid at camp?"

𝄢

Violet tore at the surface of Lake Coldwater with a double-sided paddle. Her arms ached. They'd been canoeing in uneven circles for what felt like hours. Violet checked her watch: it had only been ten minutes. The canoe wobbled, and Violet grabbed the edges for support, nearly dropping the paddle.

"We're fine," Kelly said. "But forward strokes. Let's get to the other side of the lake."

"I *am* doing forward strokes." Violet steadied herself again and waited for Kelly's signal.

"No those are J strokes. You're hooking your paddle out like the letter J. It's why we keep veering left and right."

"I'm trying not to splash you."

"Go ahead and splash me. I'd rather we go forward."

"But it's Lake Coldwater. The water's, you know, cold." Violet turned back and smiled. She was trying to play this as cool as she could, but really she was a terrible partner. The other kids had been paddling circles around them, and thanks to Violet, they had already suffered one collision. Fortunately, nobody had gone overboard. Violet squeezed her orange life vest to convince herself of its buoyancy.

"Just keep paddling, Black. I'm gonna make something of you. We are winning the canoe race at the end of this week. Synchronized. One, two, three."

Violet tried to follow Kelly's voice and the sound of her paddle. "Would this be easier if I was in back so I could watch you?" Violet asked.

"I'd rather watch *you*, so I can see when you're making mistakes, J Stroke Girl."

Violet groaned.

"Your paddle should make a line straight across. Watch the ripples in the surface. If they're curving away from the boat, we're not going straight."

After a few minutes, Violet started to notice how her strokes were influencing the direction of the boat. Staying in tune with Kelly's rhythm, she paid close attention to the angles of her strokes, and soon they were moving in a perfect line.

"Now you've got it!" Kelly exclaimed. "Keep it up, just like this. When we get closer to the other shore, we'll want to make a left turn. That's where those J's come in handy."

Violet took a relaxed breath. Aside from the strain on her arms, canoeing wasn't so bad. A cool breeze delivered the scent of pine and fresh water. A loon warbled in the distance. She could get used to this.

"Looooo-zer!" Becky and Ronny's canoe glided alongside theirs. Becky's T-shirt had "LOL" emblazoned across the chest in hot pink graffiti. "Ohmygod! Kelly Powers always, always, always comes in first at the canoe races. Like every single year. But, ohmygod!" She broke down into a fit of giggles.

Ronny scoffed. "Have you ever even *been* on a boat before, Black?"

Violet paused to consider. "I took a tour of the Queen Mary in Long Beach once."

"I'm talking about a boat, not a queen." Ronny rolled her eyes.

Becky leaned over to Kelly. "You know, we're both really good. If *we* were partners, our cabin would win."

"Sorry, Becky," Kelly said. "I'm already paired with Violet."

"But you *never* lose!" Becky looked Violet up and down. "She's *really* bad."

Kelly shrugged. "She'll get better. Thanks."

"Whatever!" Becky shoved her paddle against Kelly and Violet's canoe and launched her own boat forward. Violet grabbed both edges as the momentum rocked their boat. Her paddle slipped into the water. "You dropped something!" Becky and Ronny laughed as they glided away.

"Thanks, princess," Violet muttered. The paddle drifted away. Violet reached as far as she could.

"Hey, sit down, Vi," Kelly said. "I'll move us closer, you don't want to fall--"

"Heads up!" Becky screeched.

Violet felt a splash of cold water. She lurched forward and banged her elbows. The canoe tipped and tottered. Her forearms dunked into the icy water. Kelly grabbed her waist and steadied them.

Becky and Ronny snickered.

Icy streams ran down Violet's arms and dripped onto her shorts. Almost an inch of water was pooled at the base of their canoe. She scanned the lake. Naturally, there had been no counselor nearby to witness the incident. Back on the dock, Sassy reclined in a lawn chair; a wide brim hat covered her eyes.

"Glad we have such responsible counselors," Violet said. "Is it possible to get in trouble for *anything* here?"

"It's just water," Kelly offered.

"No. It's cold, dirty lake water that I almost fell into."

"It's cold, but it's not that dirty."

"And we'll be living with those girls for the next six weeks?"

"'Fraid so."

"Just trying to keep score." Violet sighed. "You know, you *could* switch partners. I mean I'd be pretty insulted if you paired up with Becky, but you don't have to take pity on me."

"I consider it a challenge. I train you; we win. Extra glory."

Violet smiled. "I could use some of that optimism."

Kelly maneuvered them towards Violet's floating paddle, then pulled it closer with her own. She fished it out and handed it to Violet.

Violet took the dripping paddle in both hands and faced forward. "All righty. Back on the horse." She inhaled through her nose and tried to regain that brief moment of Zen she'd almost enjoyed.

A coarse scream cut across the lake, "Sacrificial lambs!" An old woman with wiry gray hair and a green cloak shouted from the opposite shore. "Monsters! Send these children home! Monsters, all of you!"

"Who . . . is . . . that?" Kelly said.

"I don't know," Violet said, "but let's get closer."

"Closer? Are you crazy? Let's stay here!"

"Run, children! Leave this place! These cursed woods!" The woman made sweeping gestures with her cloak to usher them away.

Violet paddled forward. "I want to get a good look at her face."

"No!" Kelly halted them with a powerful backwards stroke.

The woman wailed, "Sacrifices! Sacrifices!"

"Is this a joke?" Kelly asked.

Violet glanced back. On the camp shore, counselors were hastily climbing into canoes and heading onto the water. "If it's a joke, I don't think the counselors are in on it." The counselors blew their whistles and waved orange cones, signaling for all campers to return.

"We gotta go back in." Kelly started to turn the canoe by herself. "Come on!"

"I want to hear what she has to say."

"She's crazy! Who cares what she has to say?"

The woman continued to moan and shout, but the junior counselors' whistles were drowning out her words. The other campers were all close to shore by now.

"Hey! Ms. Purple Hair!" Sassy pulled alongside their canoe in a yellow kayak. She gasped for breath, her face blue with exhaustion. Violet suspected this might be the hardest Sassy had worked in a long time.

"You okay, Sassy?" Violet asked. "You look a little fatigued."

"I'm fine!" she snapped. "Get back to shore!" She waved an orange cone in front of Violet's face. "Are you blind?"

"Sorry," Violet said. "I'm nervous. I'm not very good at canoeing, and Kelly was doing her best."

Violet snuck one last glance at the opposite shore. The woman took off into the trees as a small fleet of counselors closed in on her location.

Sassy blew her whistle, glared, and pointed to the camp side dock. Violet started to cooperate, but she maintained eye contact with Sassy. "Who's that lady?"

"Some nut who lives down the road. 'Repent and be saved,' all that garbage."

"She didn't say repent and be saved," Violet said.

Sassy scowled. "Get back to shore!"

Violet and Kelly turned their canoe around and made their way back. Most of the other kids were already tying up their boats and climbing ashore. "Were the counselors here always this nice, Kelly?" Violet asked once they had enough distance from Sassy.

Kelly remained silent.

"Your silence says to me 'this summer is off to a weird start,'" Violet suggested.

"I'd say so," Kelly said.

7

Violet and Hector sat in the office lobby beneath the antlers of a mounted buck. "And what color eyes did he have?" Violet asked.

Hector sighed. "I already told you, his eyes glowed. They glowed so bright I could see everything around me, like his head was full of fire. And with that pointy mouth and everything, he was like a jack-o-lantern. Like an eight-eyed, glowing, jack-o-spider-bag-head man."

"Spider?"

"Spiders have eight eyes."

Violet nodded. From four to five in the afternoon there were no activities scheduled. With most of the kids out playing sports or hanging out at their cabins, the office was pretty much deserted. It seemed like a good place for her to get more details from Hector.

"I already told you all of this." Hector shook his head. "And I don't really like talking about it. And I'm not sure you really believe me." He tossed his hands in the air.

"Well I don't think you believe that my dad and I are really paranormal investigators. So we're even." Violet had been taking notes on a small pad of paper. She finished up a rough sketch of an eight-eyed, jack-o-lantern-grinned face.

"I never used to believe in ghosts," Hector said. "Except now I have to."

"Stick with me, buddy. We'll get to the bottom of it one way or the other." Hector's story was consistent each time he told it. The only thing she hadn't done was compare his account to the traditional story told at camp. What was different about Hector's Happy Harry versus the legend?

It occurred to her that she'd only heard the story once, from Gary. With legends, people put their own spin on the tale when they tell it aloud. It was starting to sound unlikely that Gary had anything to do with the attack. But there was one key detail Hector hadn't touched on: Harry supposedly whistled a happy tune.

Violet didn't want to lead her witness. She worded her question carefully. "Did you hear anything unusual before you saw Happy Harry?"

Hector's eyes widened. "There *was* whistling before it happened. But I thought it was just kids nearby. I guess it was him."

"Do you remember the tune? Could you whistle it for me?"

"Um," Hector looked away. "I can't really whistle, but I do remember it."

"That's fine," Violet said. "Just hum. Or sing it with 'dees' or 'doos' or something."

Hector took a breath. "Do, do, do, do, do, doooo, do, do, doooo, do, do, dooo."

Violet could make no melodic sense of his stilted "doos." She fought the urge to laugh but couldn't suppress a grin. Finally, she broke down. "Oh wow, Hector, you can't carry a tune at all, can you?"

"Well I'm *trying*!" He stared indignantly, but as Violet's laughter continued, he eventually joined in. "Okay, I'm no good at singing. I'm no good at anything!"

"Sorry! It's fine." Violet regained her composure. "But there *was* whistling in the woods?"

Hector nodded.

"Would you recognize the tune if you heard it?"

"Definitely. It's really common music. It's in a bunch of cartoons and stuff. You hear it all the time."

Violet had never heard *anything* like the sounds that Hector had just made. But the other night Gary had whistled the march from "Peter and the Wolf." It was common enough, and if it was the same song that Hector heard, there might be a connection to Gary after all. "Was this the music you heard?" Violet whistled a few bars.

Hector listened, and then shook his head. "Nope. It's that other one. You know, it's in all the scary cartoons. Do, Do, Do, Do, Do, Do, Do, Do, Do, Do, Doooooooooooooo!"

Violet broke into laughter again.

Beneath his glare, Hector seemed just as amused by his inability to produce melody. "Oh, shut up. I'm *trying*!"

"I know you are. That's part of what's funny."

Hector sighed. "If I had internet, I could get an app that would tell me exactly what the song is."

"There's a computer lab, right?"

Hector sighed. "Yeah, where I can email my parents or go to dumb kid-friendly websites. I need *real* internet: videos, and music, and funny websites, and social networking."

"Who needs those things when you have canoes?" Violet said. "But I'll bet we *could* gather more info about Happy Harry online. If it is a local legend, and not just a camp story, there could be news articles or blogs. It would at least be a start. Let's check out the lab and see what we can find."

Hector shook his head. "Don't bother. Everything is search protected. We can email people and use encyclopedias, but that's it. If the web address doesn't end in dot edu or dot org, forget it."

"Hmm," Violet's eyes moved across the lobby to a closed staff door.

"What are you looking at?"

"Camper computers are restricted, but I'll bet the counselors have real internet." She gave Hector an imploring look.

"You think we're going to sit in Gary's office, unnoticed, long enough to do online research? That's crazy."

"I know you don't want to get in trouble, but--"

Hector lowered his voice, "Just get me the wireless password. I have a netbook, and there's a signal, but it's secured."

"Wait, what?"

"These outdoorsy counselors aren't big on e-security. The password's going to be on the desk calendar or in one of the top drawers on a little piece of paper. With that, I could do research back at my cabin all night long."

Violet crossed her arms. "Hector Chang, you are a techno-renegade, aren't you?"

"Hey you were the one talking about sneaking into the office! I was just going along--"

"Why didn't you tell me *sooner*? I'm going to put you to so much good use!" Violet stood and surveyed the lobby. The receptionist had been gone for the past fifteen minutes. She knew Gary and most of the counselors were out and about. She could only hope they left the office unlocked for convenience.

She turned back to Hector. "Keep an eye out. If you see someone coming, distract them. Make a lot of noise and try to get them to go outside with you."

"How am I going to do that?"

"Tell them you have something important to show them."

"What do I show them?"

"Tell them there's a snake in your cabin. Whatever."

"What kinds of snakes live in the area?"

"Hector! Stop overthinking this. Just get rid of them. Make noise, so I know to bail. Hopefully, it won't come to that."

"Okay, okay."

Violet strode towards the closed office door. She slowly turned the knob and pushed the door in. The interior was dark. She gave Hector a thumbs up and slipped inside.

Violet secured the door behind her. The fifteen-by-ten-foot office housed only a single desk, a file cabinet, and an old gray photocopier. Against the far corner, a door labeled "supply closet" jutted into the room. Apparently, Gary didn't share this space with anyone.

Find a password and get out, she thought. She scoured the surface of the desk. A desk calendar lay beneath the keyboard as Hector had predicted, but Gary hadn't written anything on it except for little circles every few days.

She fumbled through the top drawers of the desk. Sure enough, under a box of staples a small yellow post-it poked out. She removed it and read top to bottom: "July17fun, gmatthews@coldwater.org, ~~fortyfour44~~, fortyfive45."

Jackpot!

Violet spotted a piece of paper taped to the wall above Gary's computer monitor. It was the same hiking map they had in the lobby, except this one had a big red "X" just north of the lake and the number twelve. Next to the X was one word: cemetery.

She carefully unstuck the map from the wall and took it, along with Gary's post-it, to the copier. The copier hummed and spat out a copy of the map, minus a square in the lower left corner where she'd attached the password post-it. She returned the original post it to the drawer under the box of staples and then taped the map back to the wall, pressing hard to ensure it stuck again.

She folded her copy into her pocket then grabbed the doorknob just in time to hear Hector shouting. "Hey Gary! I need to talk to you, and it's *really* important!"

"Shoot!" Violet whispered. She glanced around the room for a hiding spot, but there weren't many options. She tried the closet, but it was locked. She panicked and dove under Gary's desk. With luck, Hector would get Gary to follow him outside, and she could make a break for it in a minute.

No such luck. Gary opened the door to his office and flicked on the lights. Violet tucked herself as tight under the desk as possible.

"I'm sorry you're not having a good time, champ," Gary said. "But you know your mom and dad can't come get you, so why don't we make the best of a potentially *good* situation!" Gary passed the desk. His keys jingled as he opened the supply closet Violet had just failed to hide in. If it hadn't been locked, he would have found her immediately.

"But the Tuckers are really mean, and I don't want to be a snitch or anything. I just, um . . . I just was hoping that you could teach me some things . . . about standing up for myself," Hector rambled.

"Huh. Well, that's good." Gary rummaged through the closet, keeping the door only partway open. He didn't sound too interested in anything Hector had to say.

Hector stammered from the doorway. "Maybe you could take me to a group of other kids and introduce me, because I'm not . . . very good at making friends?"

Violet rolled her eyes. Hector's requests sounded less sincere than his musical performance. But at least he was starting to ask for things that might lure Gary away.

"You know what, kid?" Gary's super happy voice faltered just a bit. "I'll be with you in just a minute. Why don't you take a seat out there?"

After a long silence, the door closed. *Great!* Violet thought. *Hector bailed.* She clutched her mother's ankh. *Please don't let Gary find me under his desk, please, oh please.*

Gary shut and locked the closet. He pulled his office chair back. *He's sitting down,* Violet thought. *He's going to kick me and find me with a photocopy of his personal information. And my excuse will be what exactly?*

"I hate this stupid camp!" Hector screamed from outside. "I hate the kids! I hate the counselors! I want to go home! I hate everyone!"

Gary rushed out, leaving the door wide open.

Violet heard Gary's voice shouting over Hector's outside. She made a break for it. She rolled out from under the desk and darted into the lobby.

Just outside the lobby doors, Gary had his hands on Hector's shoulders. A group of kids and counselors had gathered. Hector continued to shout. Finally, he saw Violet out of the corner of his eye.

"I need you to settle down, big time!" Gary snapped at Hector. "If you're going to be causing problems and going against the grain every day, then I guarantee you won't be having *any* fun." Gary strained to keep his upbeat attitude. "It's a prison of no fun! And you're your *own* warden!"

Violet wanted to laugh at that, but she felt too bad that Hector had just made a spectacle of himself again. Only this time, he had taken a bullet for her.

Violet circled to the left and approached Gary and Hector. She tried to appear like she was coming from a direction other than the office. "Hector! How many times do I have to tell you that you need to calm down, and that you have friends, and that you're just homesick and everything's going to be fine!" She turned to Gary. "Right, Gary? Lots of fun stuff going on, and he's all cooped up inside!"

Gary gave her a funny look, but she couldn't tell if it was suspicion or "this girl with the purple hair is starting to get really annoying."

"Hec, come on. Let's go for a walk or something. Clear your head." Violet tugged at his arm.

Gary grabbed Hector's shoulder. "No. You sir are having a talk with me. One-on-one. Right now." Gary gave Violet a dirty look. Hector shot her a "you owe me" glance as he was dragged back into the office.

❀

Later that night back at cabin 6, Hector piloted his netbook from the top bunk.

"So when Gary drags kids into his office for a 'one-on-one,' what happens next?" Violet asked. "Does phony, lame-pun Gary melt away and turn into . . ."

Hector glared from behind his monitor.

"I was going to say the Big Bad Wolf."

Hector went back to typing. "It's fine. He's no Happy Harry. Just gave me this 'three strikes you're out' speech. But I'm not sure what he's threatening me with; I *want* to go home. Maybe I'll throw some more fake tantrums and see where it gets me."

"Hey Hector," Violet said. "Thanks for saving my skin. I'm sorry you--"

"Made an idiot of myself? No big deal. I'm used to it." He stopped typing. "Yes!"

"You got internet?"

"Try to keep up, Violet," Hector said. "Wireless was accessed the second I powered up. That first password on Gary's note gives us full internet access. But here's the cool part." He turned his netbook around. The banner of the website read "Camp Coldwater." A schedule of events lay beneath.

"You got on the camp website? Good job. I want to find articles about Happy Harry, though."

"Look closer. This is the Camp Coldwater *employee* site, and I'm logged in . . ." Hector pointed to a user name in the upper right corner: Gmatthews. "As Gary!"

"You are a bad boy, Hector Chang." Violet wagged her finger. "Seriously, don't muck with Gary's emails, we want to keep a low profile. Just do a search on our Mr. Harry. Or do that music app thing you were talking about."

"Relax," Hector said. "I'm like an e-ninja. He'll never know I was here. Best part is, that post-it? It had Gary's old password that he crossed off. Fortyfour44. Letters and digits. When the camp forced him to update, he just went one number up to Fortyfive45. If Gary changes his password again, it'll be Fortysix46. Not the worst system for a password, but kinda defeats the point when you write it down for anyone to find."

Violet climbed over the side of the top bunk and watched the screen. Hector clicked various links: human resources, learning tools, emergency protocols.

"Okay, I'm impressed," she said. "But seriously, Hector, why do we need access to all this? If you start editing the payroll, I'm going to consider you an actual threat to society."

"Here's why." Hector brought up a grid of times, numbers, and activities in a new window. "If I have enough lead time, I could change the daily schedule so that I don't have to show up for any stupid sports. I could just hang out at my cabin."

"Except the activities are listed by cabin *number*. So any activity you took yourself out of, you'd have to remove the Tucker Triplets as well."

"Huh," Hector rubbed his chin. He looked dignified lost in thought. It reminded Violet of her dad. "I'll figure something out."

"I don't doubt you will." Violet tapped Hector on the shoulder. He glanced away from the glowing screen. "I seem to recall, on *multiple* occasions, you saying that you weren't good," Violet paused for dramatic effect, "at *anything!*"

"Well I'm good at computers and stuff, I guess." Hector shrugged.

Violet hit him on the arm. "No more complaining about your supposed lack of skills!"

"Ow!" Hector turned his attention back to the screen. "Hey, it's almost ten. The Tuckers will be back soon. I'm going to power this down and hide it. Otherwise, they'll be all interested in how I'm getting online and probably break this expensive netbook over my head." He shut the computer and put it aside. "But once they're asleep, I'll do some research."

"You rock." Violet handed him her notepad and a pen. "Take detailed notes. If you find anything really good, bookmark it and show me tomorrow."

"You're the boss." Hector saluted.

Violet hopped down off the bed and headed for the door.

"Hey Violet," Hector called out. "Be careful walking back."

"I'll be fine, buddy. Lay low before those three lug heads show up. I'll catch you tomorrow. Don't go editing schedules or anything that'll get Gary's attention. I'll know!" She aimed the flashlight beam at his face.

Hector held out his hands in protest. "I'll be good. Promise."

"See ya!" Violet headed into the night. Other kids who had been out by the campfires were already making their way back. She heard the Tuckers guffawing like apes as they made their way towards cabin 6. She kept her head down.

"Tomorrow, Brant has to pair up with Chang all day," one of them, presumably Trent, ordered.

"Then you take Wednesday!" Brant protested.

"By Wednesday, Happy Harry will've chopped him into a hundred pieces." Their laughter faded as they moved out of earshot.

She assumed the Tuckers didn't really believe in Happy Harry, or they wouldn't be joking about Hector being chopped up. They were jerks, but hopefully not actual psychopaths.

Violet gazed across the starlit field towards the trees where Hector had seen Harry. The night was exactly the same except for a brighter moon. Crickets chirped. She approached the trees. Soft frog croaks and crackling campfire carried from the lakefront.

She wasn't sure what she was looking for exactly. She had returned here earlier in the day, and the footprints from the other night were gone. But the singed notch in the tree remained.

She wanted to stand on that spot again and picture what Hector saw. She turned her flashlight on to ensure her footing as she made her way through the foliage. Then she emerged onto the trail and flashed her light in both directions. No campers. No counselors. No anybody.

In her mind, she ran through the records of strange and terrifying things she'd seen while traveling with her dad. Full blown apparitions. Vampires. Werewolves. A reanimated mummy. Demons. Horrible, powerful, dangerous beings most people never encounter.

So what exactly was Happy Harry? He didn't sound like a ghost. According to the story, he sold his soul to the Devil and just started killing for him. And with each kill he enjoyed his heinous deeds more and more. But how old was he? How long had he been killing? And at what point, if any, did he die?

Gary had marked a cemetery on the photocopied map. If Harry was dead, maybe his grave was there.

She stared down the path and pictured the map. The hiking path wound around the lake. It would, in theory, eventually reach Gary's cemetery. If there was a way for Hector to erase them from the daily schedule, it would allow enough time to explore the path, unsupervised, during daylight.

Then again, how could she be sure that Happy Harry didn't stalk the woods when the sun was out? *Not every creature bumps exclusively in the night,* she thought.

Violet started to cut back through the trees, when she heard it: an eerie whistling to a spooky, familiar tune. She couldn't place it, but she knew instantly that it was the same tune Hector had failed to replicate. She clutched her ankh and turned slowly. An orange glow advanced down the trail. A tall, shadowy man strolled amidst the fiery ambiance. He held a long object in one hand.

The whistling continued. The figure stopped about thirty yards away and faced camp. Hairs bristled on the back of Violet's neck.

Instinct kicked in. She bolted through the forest. Her heart pounded as she cut across the field. She didn't look back. *People who look back never like what they see,* she told herself.

She reached the front door of cabin 28, opened it, pulled herself inside and slammed the door shut, blocking it with her back. She panted.

"Oh, *my* God! Please knock if you're going to barge in like a crazy person!" Becky rolled her eyes and went back to brushing her platinum hair.

"Sorry." Violet started to catch her breath. "I'll knock . . . next time." She couldn't be happier to be inside her cabin with snotty but non-murderous Becky.

"Everything okay?" Kelly eyed her suspiciously.

"Yeah, what are you up to, freako!" Ronny was painting her nails on the floor beneath the back window. Violet couldn't help but picture Happy Harry crashing through the window, reaching for her. She didn't find it the least bit funny or satisfying.

"You know, it's getting late you guys. I think they'll be doing a lights out check soon." She stared at Ronny, obliviously brushing nail polish along her pink toes. *Maybe you should move away from the window,* she wanted to say.

"It's not even ten-thirty!" Ronny scoffed.

Violet discretely locked the door. She maneuvered to the front window and studied the empty field. It didn't look like anything had followed her. No trace of Happy Harry or his jack-o-lantern glow.

Violet stayed up half the night watching the window. By the middle of the night, she had a good feeling that whatever Happy Harry was, he seemed not to wander too far from the forest path. Just like in the story.

Violet awoke before the other girls the next morning and took a walk. Sunlight gleamed through the trees. Loons sang from the lake. She couldn't be totally sure if Happy Harry was nocturnal yet, but under the bright blue sky, she certainly felt safer.

She crossed the field and worked her way through the patch of woods, back to the spot where she had seen Harry. A tall oak tree lay across the path. Triangular gashes showed it had been chopped down.

Violet's heart pounded. A message had been carved into the tree's trunk. Sharp letters forged by the edge of a hot blade spelled out: "I SAW YOU!"

9

All morning, Happy Harry's note smoldered in Violet's mind. The message was loud and clear. "I saw you" didn't just mean that he'd physically seen her. It meant "I saw a kid who thinks she's smarter than me, and I'm going to prove her wrong."

Happy Harry knew Violet had been looking for him. Furthermore, he knew she would come back to that same spot in the morning. Otherwise, why leave a message?

Violet's dad had once explained that there were essentially two kinds of spirits: those who didn't fully understand their own actions and those who did. The ones who didn't were usually ghosts lost in a hopeless vicious cycle, replaying traumatic events. They had unfinished business, and the trouble they caused the living was incidental.

The other spirits were demons who deliberately tormented people and reveled in hateful deeds. They preyed upon the suffering of others. Harry worked for the Devil and derived pleasure from murder. He was going to be the worst kind of supernatural adversary.

Up until she had seen Harry with her own eyes, the investigation had felt more like fun and games. A chance for Violet to flex her ghost hunting muscles without Dad to shelter her.

Now she had to admit: She was scared. This was exactly the kind of case that her dad would forbid her from getting involved in. "This one's not for the faint of heart," she could almost hear him saying. "When I get back, I promise I'll tell you every last detail."

If Violet's dad knew every last detail of this case so far, he'd be on the next plane back to the States to rescue her. But Violet wasn't quite that scared. She could prove herself to him. At the end of the summer, she wanted to tell him all about how she'd handled Happy Harry like a pro. Then maybe next year it would be back to business as usual.

After another round of canoeing and a game of baseball, in which Violet struck out every at bat and Kelly hit two home runs, it was time for lunch. Kelly finished early and decided to take a jog. "You comin'?" she asked.

Violet held her hands up in surrender. "Kelly, I could never keep up with you in a million years. You're not burned out from paddling canoes, and running, and the hundreds of other things we did this morning?"

Kelly shook her head. "Once you get into the groove of physical activity, you'll learn to love it, Violet Black."

"Forced immersion. Classic brainwashing technique. I choose to spend lunch sitting down. But have fun." Violet waved goodbye.

As Kelly headed out, Hector crossed her path with his netbook case slung over his shoulder and a big smile on his face. "I found some stuff," he said.

"Excellent!" Violet said. "Hand over the case file."

"Case file?"

"That little notebook I gave you."

"You actually wanted me to take notes?"

Violet rolled her eyes. "What did you find?"

Hector started to take out his netbook, but Violet stopped him. "Not here. You don't want the counselors to know you're getting online. Tell me now, show me later."

"Coldwater Creek Library has a news database that goes back to the 1940s, so I searched for anything Happy Harry."

"And? Big urban legend, right? Not just the camp but the whole town?"

"Well, no. The local papers turned up nothing."

Violet slumped in her seat. "Huh." That couldn't be right. She had seen Harry with her own eyes last night.

"But . . ." Hector said.

"But is good, go on."

"But when I did a *general* search, I did find a few mentions of the Happy Harry story on some blogs and websites. More or less the same story. Harry's wife died. He gets all depressed. Deals with the Devil to be happy again. Kills his kids. Haunts the woods."

Violet nodded. "So we have no new information?"

"Not really, but it got me thinking. One of the guys writing this ghost blog grew up in a nearby town. So I started searching databases from the libraries of neighboring towns."

"How late were you up exactly?"

"3:30? 4:00? Who cares? I found a few articles that got printed around October from the '90s until pretty recently."

"They all reported the same story?"

Hector nodded.

"So we know the Happy Harry Legend is pretty consistent," Violet said. "No major variations."

"Not just that, but don't you think it's weird?" Hector asked.

Violet shrugged. "What part of the story *isn't* weird?"

"No, I mean why do the neighboring towns talk about the story . . ."

"But not the actual town the story takes place in. Why doesn't Coldwater Creek take pride in its local legend?" Violet thought aloud. That *was* a good question. Hector was better at this than she had expected.

"Hate to say it, Hec. But normally that means you're dealing with a little town that has a dark secret. Most places--hotels, towns, restaurants--enjoy having a fun ghost story to attract visitors. Sometimes the story is fake. Sometimes it's real, but the ghost is pretty harmless. But when you've got a deep, dark secret, usually the locals are uncooperative. None-of-your-business-blokes, my dad calls them."

"Okay," Hector said. "Then why, every stupid summer, do I always have to hear that dumb story over and over? If the locals don't like to tell people about Harry, how come the camp does?"

"Probably because, like the kids, most counselors aren't from around here. They just work here during the summer. This is the first summer since you've been coming here that anything really weird has happened, right? The first time a camper has claimed to see Harry."

"As far as I know."

The more Violet thought about the situation, the less sense it seemed to make. The locals were hush-hush about the truth, but the camp embraced the story because, up until this year, it had seemed harmless.

What changed? What was different about this year? Kelly had mentioned this was Gary's first summer as head counselor. In fact, she'd heard other kids remark that it was mostly new faces. The mystery kept pointing back to the staff, but Violet had seen Harry with her own eyes. He certainly didn't seem like some guy in a mask.

"Hey Hector," Violet asked. "Could you please hum that tune for me again? The one Harry whistled?"

Hector blushed. "You know I can't do it."

"Just try. I won't laugh this time, promise."

Hector hummed. After a moment, Violet whistled along with him, the same tune she had heard the night before.

Hector's eyes lit up, and he nodded at Violet's recognition. "I must have done better that time! Do you know the song?"

Violet wasn't sure how to respond.

Hector's face melted into dread. "You heard him, didn't you?"

Violet nodded.

"You *saw* him?"

Violet sighed. "Um . . ."

"I told you to be careful! You didn't go into the woods last night by yourself, did you?"

"I've been doing this a long time, Hector."

"That guy has an ax! He wants to chop kids into bits! Are you crazy?"

Other kids were starting to stare at their table. "Hector! Shhh. Inside voices, 'kay?"

Hector folded his arms. "Do you know the song?"

"I recognize it, but I don't know the name," she said. Hector had been correct. It was classical music Violet had heard in movies and cartoons, but she didn't know the composer. *Dad would know this,* she thought.

"I kind of want to say Mussorgsky," she suggested. "Night on Bald Mountain." She ran through that in her head for a few seconds. "No, that's not it. This is going to drive me nuts. If I could find out the song that might at least give us some idea of how old Happy Harry *isn't.* Could provide a few clues about the kind of person he was too."

"I don't know anything about music," Hector said. "But I know that song. Next chance I get, I'll download some music recognition software. What else do you want me to look into?"

Violet smiled. Hector was really getting into his new research job. She lowered her voice, "Gary's map says there's a cemetery north of the lake. Try to find out what you can about that. And let's both try to come up with a way to edit that schedule."

"I thought I wasn't supposed to do that."

"Well, desperate times and desperate measures and all that. I want to check out that cemetery, and I'd rather do it in daylight."

"Song, cemetery, schedule. Anything else?"

"That's it for now, Boy Wonder." Violet checked her watch and made a disgusted face. "We've got a whole afternoon of sports, aloof counselors, and bratty campers ahead of us. You should probably put that netbook someplace safe and get moving."

"Right." Hector stood, but before he left he looked Violet square in the eyes. "You're supposed to be some kind of expert about stuff like this, right?"

Violet reluctantly nodded. Her dad was the real expert; she was still learning.

"But I'll bet you didn't get a *really* good look into that thing's eyes, did you?"

She didn't respond. He was right. She'd only seen Harry from a distance through trees.

"Please promise me you won't go after him by yourself. I know I'm not the ghost hunter, but we don't really know enough about what we're dealing with yet, right?"

"No, we don't," Violet said. *Actually I do know enough,* Violet thought. *Enough to know I was stupid to go out alone last night.*

"Just be careful, okay?" Hector broke eye contact. "I really like you, you know, as a friend. And I don't have any other friends here, and I'm glad you're helping me, but . . . I don't want anything bad to happen."

Violet smiled. "You're sweet, Hector." She put her left hand over her heart and held up her right. "I Violet Black swear on the soul of my mother that I will not go after Happy Harry by myself until I know more about what's going on."

"Thanks." Hector smiled and scratched the back of his head. "Gotta go, but I'll see you later!" He darted through the rows of tables. On the way out, he grabbed three bags of chips and a bottle of cola.

"Lunch of champions," Violet said to herself. She whistled Happy Harry's painfully familiar tune beneath the chatter of her fellow campers.

10

After lunch, Violet's schedule directed her to the archery range on the north side of camp.

Sassy paced in front of fifteen foam targets. She held up a gray longbow and a wooden arrow. "This equipment is expensive. It's one bow per cabin, and everyone takes responsibility. Everybody has to wear an arm guard. If you don't, and you whip your skin," she snapped the bowstring, "don't come cryin' to me!

"Line up! Every group of four take a target. Take turns. Share. All that good stuff." Sassy motioned to a nearby table where two more junior counselors started passing out bows and quivers.

Violet raised her hand. "I've never shot an arrow before. So is there like . . . a lesson, or something?"

Sassy wiped her nose on the back of her wrist. "It's a bow and arrow. What's so difficult? Pull back and let it fly."

"That sounds safe," Violet muttered.

"It's okay," Kelly whispered. "I can teach you. I doubt Sassy's even qualified."

Becky and Ronny appeared with a longbow and quiver. "Since we went and got the bow, I get to go first," Becky announced.

"How come Ronny doesn't get to go first?" Violet asked.

"Because she gets to be," Becky thought for a moment, "the arrow-passer-outer."

"What a privilege, huh Ronny?" Violet said.

Ronny sneered. "Shut up, Black." She slapped an arm guard against Violet's chest. They all strapped the guards over their left wrists.

Violet couldn't wait to see how prim and prissy Becky handled herself with a bow and arrow. *I may have never fired a shot in my life,* Violet thought. *But I know I'm tougher than her.*

Her smile faded when Becky stepped up, took position, drew back an arrow, and let it fly into one of the inner rings of their target.

"Nice!" Ronny cheered.

Becky let another five arrows fly. All of them hit within the target. Then Ronny took a turn, doing equally well. The girls high-fived each other and strutted off to retrieve the arrows.

Violet sighed. "Looks like Becky and Ronny could be a tough act to follow. Wish me luck."

"You'll do fine," Kelly said. "Don't compare yourself to them. Most of these girls took archery lessons from Mike last year, and he was a great teacher. I was hoping he'd still be around. To be honest, I don't have the best aim either. But shooting's not so hard."

Becky and Ronny returned and passed the bow and quiver to Kelly. "See if you two can beat that." Becky raised her arms and did a little victory dance.

"Nobody's keeping score, Becky," Violet said.

"Losers don't keep score!"

Violet ignored her and watched Kelly prepare.

"Load the bow horizontal." Kelly lined a wooden arrow up, grasped it underhand, and turned the bow parallel to her body. "Raise your arms to eye level. Draw back." Kelly pulled the string back until her right hand touched her face. "You want to have an anchor point."

"Anchor point?"

"It can be anything. See how my middle knuckle is against my cheekbone? If I do that every time, I know I'll always have the same power level in my shot."

"Got it."

"These longbows don't have crosshairs, so just eyeball the shot. Think about which way the wind is blowing and use instinct. Release." Kelly let her arrow fly. It hit the outer ring. "Dang. Guess I'm out of practice."

"You hit the target," Violet said. "I'm impressed."

"I know I can get closer to that bull's-eye." Kelly prepped another arrow. "Do you follow the basics, though?" Kelly let another arrow fly. This one hit a few inches below her first shot.

"I'm following," Violet said. She watched Kelly unload a few more.

"You want to try?" Kelly offered her the bow.

Violet took a deep breath. "Sure." She held the bow like Kelly had, took an arrow, and fumbled with it.

Becky and Ronny giggled.

"Here." Kelly got behind Violet and helped her find the notch. "Clench your fingers." Kelly moved Violet's fingers around the red fletching. "Now turn vertical."

Violet tightened her grip around the arrow and held it upright.

"Higher," Kelly instructed. "Eye level."

Violet raised her arms until the wooden point of the arrow lined up with her eyes.

"But the back end too," Kelly said. "You need to find your anchor--"

"Violet sucks!" Becky screamed in her ear.

Violet jumped and released. Her arrow arched into the air and soared over the target into the trees. She turned and screamed at Becky. "If you don't shut up, the next arrow's going through your pretty little face!"

"Ooooooh, I'm so scared!" Becky snickered.

"Cut it out! Someone could get hurt," Kelly snapped. "Just ignore her, Violet. You were doing fine."

Violet loaded another arrow. She raised her arm and drew back to her cheek again. But her arms shook in frustration. She released, and her shot veered left into the forest.

"See, she's messing up on her own," Becky said.

Violet took another shot; her arrow soared just over the top of the target. She groaned.

"Try again," Kelly said. "For a first time, this isn't bad."

"Oh, it's bad," Becky insisted. "Purple Streaks is almost as pathetic at archery as she is at canoeing. Are you sure you don't want to switch partners, Kelly?"

"Positive," Kelly said.

Violet sent another arrow sailing left. She turned and glared at Becky.

Becky brushed her perfect blond hair out of her eye and shot Violet a condescending smirk. "I know we're supposed to be having fun and everything, and I'm sure there's lots of things that Violet Black is good at, like reading books, or thinking about things, or whatever. But it's dumb when the best athlete in camp is always partnering up with the worst."

"Well, how else am I supposed to *learn*?" Violet prepped another arrow.

"I don't get it," Becky continued. "Do you just pair up with losers to be nice, Kelly? You're really good. If you hung out with me, you'd be really cool too."

Kelly laughed. "Is that a fact?"

"Totally!"

Violet released another arrow that sailed too far right. "I'm comfortable being Kelly's second banana," she said, turning around again. "What do you think, Ronny? No shame being second, right?"

Ronny had been playing with a strand of frizzy red hair. She glanced up. "Huh?"

"You don't mind that Becky keeps trying to trade you for a better partner, do you?" Violet asked.

Becky glared at Violet, and then put her arm around Ronny's shoulder. "Ronny and I are total BFFs. She knows that."

Ronny said nothing.

"I'm sure you are," Violet said. She took her last shot and lodged an arrow into the foam board above the outer circle. "Hey! It didn't go in the woods that time!"

"See, you're improving." Kelly patted her shoulder.

"You'd better go find all those arrows," Ronny said. "If we're missing any, it'll be your fault."

"I'll find them," Violet said. "Relax."

She handed Kelly the bow and headed towards the trees behind the target. The red fletching of the first three arrows stood out in the grass at the edge of the woods. She ventured into the trees to find the fourth and discovered it at the base of a large oak. The fifth one had to be nearby. Violet faced the archery range and scanned the forest floor.

Suddenly, a pair of strong hands grabbed her from behind. She dropped her arrows and shouted as something dragged her into the woods.

11

The attacker's nails dug into her arms. Violet kicked and struggled, then finally managed to stomp the foot of the person behind her and elbow him in the chest. He grunted and stumbled backwards.

Violet spun around to find a cloaked figure with a ghost-faced mask, hunched in pain. He grunted, strode forward, and took a swing at Violet. Violet ducked and rolled away.

Someone else grabbed her. Violet shouted and squirmed.

"Hey! It's me!" Kelly said, holding her arm out. She helped Violet to her feet. "I came to help and heard you shout."

Violet searched frantically around them. The cloaked figure reappeared between them and the archery range. Kelly gasped. The assailant balled up his fists. "Take one more step, and I'll pound you."

Kelly stepped forward.

The ghost-faced attacker swung at her with his massive fist. Kelly ducked and punched him square in the crotch. The figure shrieked, doubled over, and held his privates. Kelly reached down and yanked the mask off his face to reveal one of the Tucker Triplets.

"Nice," Violet said. "You know the killers in horror movies usually last until act three before they get into these kinds of situations."

The Tucker tried to say something, but he could only continue his high pitched groan.

"Brent or Brant?" Violet asked.

"B-Brent," he wheezed.

"So you're Brant then. Because Trent's the alpha male, you're his henchmen, and each one of you would try to frame the other in a situation like this. Am I right?" Violet prodded him in the shoulder with her shoe.

He nodded. "Yeah. I'm Brant."

Violet peered through the trees. Somehow, not a single person from the archery range had heard the racket. That was a lot scarier than Brant's mask.

"Okay, Brant. Or Trent, or Brent, or whichever." Violet leaned into his face. "You just attacked two girls, wearing a mask, in the middle of the woods. This is the kind of thing people go to jail for. Kelly and I could be pressing all kinds of charges here."

"I was just messin' around," Brant said, finally finding the energy to sit. "I only wanted to scare you."

"Aren't you supposed to be canoeing or something?" Kelly asked.

"I ditched! So what?"

"*So* we won't tell the counselors. No pressing charges. Won't even tell other kids this incredibly sweet story about how one of the big bad Tucker Triplets got beat up by a girl." Violet patted Kelly's shoulder. "But in exchange, you guys have to stop picking on Hector Chang. Seriously. He's a harmless, mild-mannered kid. You guys are big hulking monsters, and enough is enough."

"I'll try to get them to stop, just don't tell anyone, all right?"

"No try." Violet held up her finger. "Do!"

"We're only picking on him because we're supposed to."

"What does that mean?" Violet asked.

"Trent says Happy Harry won't kill us if we're bad."

Violet searched Brant's eyes. "You don't *really* believe in that stupid story though, right?"

"I don't know." He stared into the woods.

"Look, Brant." Violet held out her hand to help him up. His weight almost pulled her onto the ground, and she gave up. "Listen. Happy Harry isn't an excuse to bully kids. It's dumb. If there was a Happy Harry, he would be killing all of us left and right, whether we were bullies, or goody-goodies, or whatever. We're all thirteen or younger right? That's innocent enough for a servant of the Devil. The best way to not get murdered by Happy Harry is to just stay out of the woods at night. End of story."

Brant looked Violet up and down. "How do you know?" He lowered his voice, "You seen him?"

Kelly and Brant both waited for an answer.

"It's just an educated guess," Violet said. "The point is: stop being a horse's behind and go find your brothers before they jump out at people and make idiots of themselves too."

Brant headed through the woods. He appeared to be hiding a limp.

"It's okay to feel pain, tough guy," Violet called as he left. "That's how we know we're alive!"

"Maybe you shouldn't push your luck by taunting ogre number two," Kelly said after Brant disappeared in the trees.

"With you by my side, I'm feeling pretty invincible. You make a good bodyguard."

"You think they'll really stop bugging Hector, or do you think you just made it worse?" Kelly asked.

Violet considered it. She had almost certainly made things worse. "You know if we're going to teach one of those three a lesson, it should be Trent. He's the leader."

Kelly took a few steps past Violet, stooped down, and found the fifth stray arrow. "You're pretty nice to Hector, considering he can be just as obnoxious as the Tuckers in his own way. What kind of lesson do you have in mind for Trent?"

"I think, perhaps, a lesson in fear is in order," Violet thought out loud. She just wasn't sure who the instructor was going to be, or whether or not the Tuckers' lesson had already begun.

12

Hector held his netbook so close to Violet's face that the screen burned her eyes. "Whistle Happy Harry's tune."

"You sure this is going to work?" Violet pulled away. The purple banner on the web browser read "Lyrieka."

"Positive. It's music recognition software. It can tell you the name of the song and the artist. But *you* have to do it because it doesn't understand when I try."

"I can't imagine why," Violet teased.

He pushed the netbook closer. "Right into the microphone."

Violet whistled the familiar, creepy song that had been stuck in her head all day. A pink loading icon swirled onscreen. Soon, a list of songs and composers appeared. "Aha!" Violet shouted. "My dad totally would have known that!"

Hector read the title that dominated the list: "In the Hall of the Mountain King?"

"That's definitely it," Violet said. "And you're right, they always use it as background music in scary cartoons."

"Let's make sure." Hector clicked his touchpad, and the same eerie tune played. Low, unassuming cello and bassoon movements opened the piece like gentle footfalls. As the music built, it gained momentum and intensity. Different instruments intruded upon the quiet repeating pattern. Growing, building, and colliding as if one note was chasing the next. The instruments moved faster and faster until the music reached an epic swell. Then it returned to its original, unobtrusive tone and ended on a high pointed note.

The piece only lasted a few minutes, but listening to it reminded Violet of a hiker walking along the forest path being pursued, chased, and overcome. And someone escaping into the night at the end. Clearly Harry's theme.

Hector sat spellbound, but after a moment, he opened a new tab in his browser and searched. "In the Hall of the Mountain King . . . composed by Edvard Grieg. It's part of a musical . . . *Peer Gynt*."

"That sounds familiar," Violet paced the cabin. "What's Grieg's nationality?"

Hector searched. "Norwegian."

"When did he compose *Peer Gynt*?"

"Um, it premiered in 1867."

"Where?"

"Copenhagen. Denmark."

Violet processed the information. "Based on the story of Happy Harry, I think it's safe to say that he lived at least a century ago. I'm not a historian or anything, but most people past 1940 probably didn't make a living chopping down trees in the forest."

"Some of them might have. People still make a living doing that," Hector said.

"I'm brainstorming here, Hec. Work with me." Violet peered out the window at the pointed pines that lined the forest path. "Harry and his family lived in the woods. Chances are they were poor immigrants. Maybe that music has special significance for Harry. Maybe his dad used to whistle it when he was a kid."

Hector shrugged. "Maybe it's just a creepy song though."

"When ghosts repeat actions, the pattern usually has some connection to who they were in life. Happy Harry isn't exactly a ghost, but according to the story, he used to be a family man. Killing makes him happy. Why would he whistle that tune while stalking the woods unless it made him happy too?"

"Yeah, I guess," Hector said. "But it's scary music. He's probably using it to scare his victims."

Violet shook her head. "He's Happy Harry, not Scary Scotty. The fact that what makes him happy makes us scared could be coincidence. We have to try to think like Harry to understand him."

"I'm not sure I know where you're going with this." Hector collapsed on Kelly's bed.

"You don't have to. Up!" Violet motioned for Hector to sit. "I need you on the keys. Come on." Violet grabbed Hector by the wrists and pulled him to his computer. "When was the phonograph invented, Hector? Or the radio? Around what time?"

"Why does this matter?" Hector said, already running a search.

"Humor me."

Hector clicked a link, scanned a page, and revealed, "The phonograph was invented in 1867. Mass produced in the 1890s." About twenty seconds later he said, "The radio was also the 1890s."

"How about broadcasting? Broadcasting of music?"

Hector read on. "Sounds like broadcasting became popular in the 1920s."

Violet reached out. "Hand me the case file."

Hector tossed her the pad of paper.

"Pen me."

Violet caught her blue clicky-pen and jotted down numbers. "Poor woodsmen like Harry don't go to see operas like *Peer Gynt*, plus he was here in America anyway. But maybe a wealthy older relative passed the tune along to him as a child. Or possibly he was listening to classical music on the radio. Either way, that means that when Happy Harry theoretically made his deal with the Devil, it was roughly between 1925 and 1935." Violet circled the dates on her pad. "Give or take."

"I guess that makes sense."

"Also, this might be a stab in the dark, but chances are Harry had a Norwegian, Swedish, or Danish sounding last name."

"How does that help?"

"Because, Research Boy . . ." She pulled out Gary's map, unfolded it, and pointed to the X. "Now we have a way of narrowing down the names on the graves in the cemetery."

"Oh." Hector paused. "Wait, what? What are we going to do once we find his grave? Dig it up? Are you crazy?"

Violet sighed. "We just want a name. We want to know more about him."

"Then what happens? I want to get rid of him, not write a report, Violet. You're the ghost hunter. How do we *stop* the ghost?"

Violet held up her finger. "I appreciate your zest for slaying things that go bump in the night, Hector. But we can't get rid of something we don't know anything about. According to the story, Happy Harry didn't even die. He just took up a contract with the Devil, started killing, and kept at it."

"Well if he didn't die, he won't have a grave then, will he?" Hector held up his own finger.

"You're so cute when you act like a know-it-all," Violet said. "Harry's wife *did* die. We're looking for *her* grave. If we find Mrs. Happy Harry, we might actually get to the bottom of the whole thing. His grief over her death started it all."

"What are we going to do? Raise her from the dead, so they can live happily ever after?"

Violet shrugged. "We'll cross that bridge when we get there."

Hector stared for a moment, and then went back to his netbook. "I'm afraid to ask if you're joking, so I'm moving to our next order of business: ditching tomorrow's activities.

"The easiest way is to put us on the sick roster. I think the counselors print their schedules while we're eating breakfast. Nurses and counselors have different schedules, so nobody will be knocking on our doors with chicken soup or anything."

"So everyone thinks you and I are sick," Violet nodded, "and we get out of activities while our bunkmates don't. That works."

"The only thing is if the Tuckers or your roommates come back during break periods, they'll see that we're not home," Hector said. "They probably won't care though."

"The Tuckers probably won't." Violet thought about Brant in the woods earlier. "Come to think of it, they're probably ditching activities left and right and barely getting into any trouble. Where was Brant this afternoon?"

Hector looked up. "Brant? They were all . . ." He made a confused face. "We were all canoeing."

Violet wasn't sure if she should tell Hector about her and Kelly threatening Brant. It might wound his pride. But she did want to know how the Tuckers were sneaking away. "It's two to a canoe, right? So two Tuckers rowed together, and the other one was with you?"

Hector shook his head. "No, I was with this other kid."

"Let me guess. There's an odd number of boys." *That would be convenient for a trio of mischievous triplets,* Violet thought. *One Tucker pulls pranks while the other two keep up the appearance of all three.*

"I never bothered to count," Hector said. "You'd think the counselors would keep an eye on them though."

Violet knew for a fact that Brant at least had snuck away successfully. "I'm not so sure about these counselors. They're not exactly highly motivated. At least Sassy and her girl counselors aren't."

"Fine with me," Hector said. "Makes it less likely we'll get caught. Just make sure your roommates don't tell."

"Huh." Violet hadn't given that enough thought. Becky and Ronny might tell if they found out. She *wanted* to explain things to Kelly. Violet didn't want to bail as a canoe partner or make Kelly worry that she was sick.

And yet the other options seemed worse. Tell her nice, normal friend that she was having a weird ghost girl adventure? Lie to Kelly and say she was sneaking off into the woods with Hector? To do what? *Not* hunt ghosts? Why else would two kids sneak away? There would be rumors circling about her and Hector almost immediately.

"I don't know what to tell Kelly," Violet finally said.

"What do you mean?"

"I mean she's really cool. I finally have a nice, normal girlfriend. If I try to trust her about this Happy Harry thing, she'll just think I'm--"

"Weird?"

"Yeah."

"Welcome to my world." Hector went back to surfing the net.

"You're a big help. The problem is if I'm honest, she won't believe me, and there's no good little white lies for this situation."

"You're Violet Black. You'll figure something out," Hector said.

The door opened and Kelly entered, sweaty from a jog. "Hey Violet, ready for dinner?" She noticed Hector on her bed. "What up, Chang? Brant Tucker give you any trouble this afternoon?"

Hector glanced curiously between the two girls. "Why Brant? Why not the other two?"

"Why anything?" Violet smiled. "Hey Hector, maybe you should put that netbook some place safe. I'll catch you later."

"Okay." He tucked his computer in its case and made his way to the door. Before he left, he said, "Oh, Kelly. Violet has something she wanted to explain to you. See you guys later!" He let the door slam as he walked off.

Kelly stared at the door, then at Violet. "What's he talking about? Did you tell him what happened with Brant?"

Violet shrugged. "He's so weird. I have no idea what he meant."

Kelly smiled and pointed between the door and Violet. "Are you and Hector Chang . . . ?"

Violet panicked. "Oh God, no! Nothing like that at all. Just buddies. Seriously, I'm like his life coach. Not even. More like a mentor. I mean, we're just friends, Kelly. Seriously, I'd tell you. No, no, no, not at all. Not in a million years. Gross."

Kelly laughed. Violet nervously laughed with her. If Happy Harry didn't get Hector, she just might bump him off herself. Why would he put her in this awkward situation?

Someone knocked at the door. Violet felt a deep pit of regret in her stomach as Hector's sad muffled voice came through. "I forgot my charger."

"Oh." Violet found the adapter to Hector's computer on Kelly's bed. She brought it to the door and started to open it.

Hector's hand reached in. "Just give it to me, and I'll go."

"Hector . . ."

"Just give it to me, thanks." He took the cord and shuffled away.

Violet's face burned with shame. She turned to Kelly. "Do you think he heard me say all that?"

Kelly gave a tight-lipped shake of her head and shrugged. It was a polite way of saying "definitely."

Violet collapsed on Kelly's bottom bunk. "Oh man, am I an idiot!" Talk about wounded pride. Everything she had done to boost Hector's confidence since they met, crushed by ten seconds of thoughtless rambling. *Not in a million years,* her words echoed in her mind. *Gross!* She might as well have ripped his heart out.

"He'll get over it," Kelly said. "You're one of the only people at this whole camp--actually, one of the only people I know--who's nice to that kid."

Violet covered her face with Kelly's pillow. "You're not making me feel better."

"Sorry. But face facts, Vi. If Hector had some kind of crush on you, it was better that you laid it out plain and simple. It's not the worst thing that's going to happen to him this summer."

Violet considered that for a moment. "Let's hope it is."

13

Violet watched a fly crawl along the maroon colored hotdog on her plate. "I don't know why I keep thinking I'm going to like these." The fly rubbed its legs together, then buzzed off to another table. "The insects won't even eat it."

Kelly had somehow managed to scrounge up a chicken breast, broccoli, and a side of yogurt and nuts.

"Where are you getting all that healthy food? I never see any of that stuff out at the," she gestured towards the metal serving pans lined up by the cafeteria, "the outdoor serving area!"

"The counselors get special meals, so I asked if I could have one too." She took a spoonful of yogurt.

"They'll make kids special dinners? That sounds like the opposite of the way we usually get treated."

"My dad wrote a doctor's note."

"I keep forgetting that this is not your first summer of rubber hotdogs. You adapted. Good for you." She took her hotdog out of the bun and waggled it at Kelly. "I swear I am never ever letting my dad send me here again. But if by some horrible accident he does, I am definitely getting one of those doctor note arrangements."

She tossed her dog over by a tree stump. Some manner of wild animal was bound to enjoy it. She slumped onto her elbows and started to eat her empty bun.

"Here." Kelly cut her chicken and deposited half on Violet's plate.

"Have I told you lately that I love you?" Violet wrapped her half a chicken breast in her stale bun and savored a big juicy bite. "Mmm, unbelievable."

"It's just overcooked chicken."

Violet swallowed. "Everything's relative."

"Hey!" Sassy loomed over their table. She pointed to where Violet had discarded her hotdog. "Don't waste food! Children are starving in . . . you know . . . one of those loser countries!"

"I don't know of any countries where the children eat rubber," Violet said.

Sassy stooped down and glared at Violet. "You've got a mouth on you, purple-puss." A medallion slipped out of Sassy's shirt and dangled around her neck: a five-pronged star in a circle, with the tip pointing down.

"Well now," Violet said. "That's pretty."

It swayed back and forth for just a moment before Sassy stuffed it back under her collar. But Violet had gotten a good enough look.

"Where did you get that charm, Sassy?" Violet asked.

"My granny gave it to me. What's it to ya?" Sassy pointed to the tree stump. "Pick up that hotdog, and put it in the trash where it belongs." She stormed off.

"No problem." As Violet fetched her discarded rubber dog and tossed it in the nearest trash can, she kept an eye on the surly counselor doing her rounds. *You just got a lot more interesting, Sassy,* she thought.

Sassy's "granny's medal" was an inverted pentagram, a symbol associated with ancient magic. The downward pointing star usually meant Satanism. But Violet wasn't sure in Sassy's case. *She could be a skilled practitioner of dark arts,* Violet pondered. *Or just a bratty college kid who's into Wicca.*

Hector passed by with a plate overflowing with burgers and chips. He ignored her, proceeded past every table, and sat alone by the lakefront. After setting his food down, he began hurling rocks into the water.

"He does not know how to skip stones," Kelly said.

"I know; it's a problem." Violet watched him sink another handful. "I can't take this. I have to clear my conscience." She stuffed the remaining morsels of chicken into her mouth.

"Do what you gotta do," Kelly said. "Just remember, that kid overreacts and loves to make a scene."

Violet wasn't sure how to take that. Sure, Kelly had known Hector longer, but the only "scenes" he'd made this week resulted from getting bullied, escaping a demonic being, and creating a diversion to save Violet's skin. "I think he's a very smart, nice guy, and he's high strung because everyone gives him a hard time."

Kelly shrugged. "Okay."

"Wish me luck."

Kelly saluted.

Violet made her way to the lake and sat in the gravel next to Hector. He pretended not to notice and hurled a big flat stone right through the surface of the water.

"You gotta give it a little spin, remember?"

"Well, I just stink at it."

She pointed to his plate. "Your chips are getting cold."

"Chips aren't hot."

"Well I would have said the burgers were getting cold, but this is Camp Coldwater. All food is inedible upon arrival."

Hector didn't even crack a smile.

"I am really, really sorry about what I said to Kelly. I panicked, and I didn't want her to get the wrong idea."

He glared at the lake. "Just leave me alone."

"Hector, please don't do this to me. I need your help with this whole Happy Harry thing. No, forget that. I need you to help me get through this horrible month at summer camp. You're smart. You're funny. You're dependable. I need friends like you."

"Whatever."

"Don't give me whatever. I'm serious. Okay, the main reason I started talking to you was because I felt bad for you, but the more I get to know you, the more I realize what a cool guy you are."

"Yeah right. You said it yourself: I'm gross."

"Well it is gross to think of my friends as my . . ." Violet had to phrase this carefully. "I'm not really the dating type, Hector. It just doesn't interest me right now. I would rather have a new friend any day, any time. Good friends are forever. Cute boys are," she took a rock and skipped it a few times until it sank, "temporary."

"Right, and I'm not cute."

"You're totally cute, Hector. But cute for some other girl someday. I want to be your buddy. Your BFF. Eventually, you'll be in high school, and you can email me for advice about what to say and do on a date. Today you're thirteen. There's plenty of time for dating and boyfriends and girlfriends later."

"I'm twelve," he said. "I got skipped ahead."

"Well that's even better. Younger *and* smarter. You have all the time in the world. Junior high stinks for people like us. That's why we need to stick together."

Hector finally made eye contact. "I didn't think you were going to date me or anything like that, Violet. I'm not stupid. You're really funny, and smart, and . . . charming."

"True, true, and true, but that doesn't mean--"

"I just thought you were cool too." He looked away. "Not cool, like popular. Cool like . . . you were a really nice person who sticks up for people and says nice things about them all the time."

"Nobody says nice things *all the time*, Hector. I blew it, okay? I'm sorry. You're not gross. Someday I would be lucky to have a nice guy like you as a boyfriend. Any girl would be."

He hurled another stone, and it plunked right through the water's surface.

"Please don't be mad at me. I can't afford it."

"Why, because you need my computer to look stuff up?"

"Because I need *friends*. We've been over this. You *are* stubborn."

"I'll still be your friend," he said. "But you're not making me feel better."

"Would it help if I sat here and said nice things about you all night long?"

"I wouldn't believe any of it."

"You're a genius. You could outsmart the guys at the Apple store. You got skipped ahead. You have handsome dark eyes and a cute smile. You went up against a demonic entity and lived to tell the tale. You're brave enough to fight back. You're a survivor."

"Fine!" Hector forced a wide fake grin. "I'm happy, just leave me alone for a little while, okay?"

Violet nodded. "Okay." She started to walk away. "Are we still sick tomorrow?"

"Yeah. Plan's still on."

"Good." Violet walked back towards the picnic tables. Now she definitely wanted to get Kelly in on tomorrow's plan. She wasn't sure she could stand exploring the woods one-on-one with forlorn, mopey Hector. She was going to need some kind of buffer. But once again, how on Earth was she supposed to broach the topic?

"Oh my God!" Ronny stood at a nearby table and pointed over the lake. A hush came over the grounds as more kids stood, gasped, and pointed. Violet turned around, half expecting Hector to be making some kind of scene after all. But he too was watching, still as a statue.

Across the water, below the pink clouds of dusk, a tall figure strolled along. His face glowed like a torch. His hand clutched a jagged-handled ax. It was Happy Harry, roaming the path on the other side of the lake, right where the old woman in green had appeared the other day.

As the murmuring crowd gave way to shocked silence, the melodic whistling of "Hall of the Mountain King" carried over the lake. Harry faced the camp. He pointed his glowing ax at them. Then he continued on and disappeared behind the southern trees. Once Harry was gone, Ronny unleashed an ear-splitting scream.

14

The next morning, Violet and Kelly waited for Hector in the trees outside camp. "I can't believe you talked me into this." Kelly slapped the back of her neck. A horsefly dropped to the forest floor. "We're totally going to get busted."

Violet was still bursting with excitement from the previous night. "Full blown apparition in front of *everybody*! My dad would never believe a sighting with this many witnesses."

"*I* don't believe it," Kelly reminded her. "I only agreed to come along because I don't want you getting lost."

"And I appreciate that. It's good to have a seasoned tour guide, even if she's a skeptic."

"Anyone can dress in a costume and wander around the woods, Violet." She slapped another horsefly on her arm. "Brant Tucker's proof of that. It was probably just him, or one of his bonehead brothers, playing a prank."

Violet shook her head. "I took inventory. All three Tuckers were accounted for at the sighting. Besides, Happy Harry is too tall and too thin."

Kelly shrugged.

"Much more interesting to me is that *none* of the counselors claimed to have seen anything. Even the ones that were nearby. And Gary. Where was he?"

"Gary showed up right afterwards to calm people down," Kelly said.

"Not right afterwards. Several *minutes* afterwards. But I agree. It would have been pretty hard to get around the lake that fast."

Hector emerged between the distant cabins. A backpack, bigger than his torso, was strapped around his waist and shoulders. He panted as he reached the trees.

"Hector, we're checking out the cemetery, not climbing Mount Everest. What is all that stuff?" Violet prodded his enormous pack, and he almost tipped backwards.

"Supplies." He steadied himself. "The netbook in case we can get a signal and need to look something up. Case file, flashlights, water, some food I stashed from dinner last night, change of clothes . . ."

Kelly raised her eyebrow. "Change of clothes? For when we see Happy Harry and you wet yourself?"

"Ha Ha!" Hector glared. "What if it rains or one of us falls into a creek or something? What if we get stuck out there for days?"

"That won't happen," Kelly said. "Besides, if you get wet, you're going to ruin that fancy computer of yours."

Hector's jaw dropped.

Kelly had a point, but it was already past breakfast. Violet didn't want to waste time. "It's fine, Hector. Next time, pack lighter. But we need to get moving."

They followed the path around the lake. Hector had timed their departure with the activity schedule, so that nobody would be hiking at the same time. When Sassy had taken the girls hiking, she had veered onto a trail that branched north of camp and looped back around, a solid fifteen minute walk.

Yet the main trail on Gary's map rounded the entire lake. The cemetery lay north of the lake. Once they'd passed the last of the camp sponsored paths, Violet had a good sense of just how far north they were going.

After twenty minutes, Hector slumped his enormous pack against a tree in exhaustion. "Five minutes guys," he panted.

Kelly glared. "I told you not to bring that stupid backpack!"

"It's fine! I just need a rest."

"You're exhausted," Kelly said. "You're slowing us down a lot."

"Who wants water?" Hector grunted as he removed his pack.

"I'll have some," Violet offered. Maybe it would help if they drank some of the weight out of Hector's supplies.

Hector removed two sport bottles from his bag. He handed one to Violet as he sucked away at the other. Kelly opened his bag and sifted through its contents.

Hector finished his long sip and unleashed a satisfied "Ah!"

"Jeez!" Kelly pulled out three identical bottles of water. "How many *gallons* of water did you bring, Chang?" She found a fourth bottle and groaned.

"Water is important for survival! People in life-or-death situations are always desperate for water."

Kelly started to dump the contents of each bottle.

"Hey!"

"The weight of this bag is *crushing* your puny body . . . because you filled it with *fifty pounds* of liquid!"

"I don't want to die of dehydration."

Kelly dumped the next bottle and gestured west. "There is a *huge* freshwater lake right there! It will not come to that."

"I like to be prepared!" Hector shouted.

"You might as well have 'prepared' by filling this bag with bricks, moron!"

Violet whistled. "Okay! Enough! Good points, Kelly. But he meant well." Violet took one last sip of water, then emptied her bottle. "How about we keep one bottle for the three of us to share, dump the rest, and lighten your load?"

Hector nodded and started to dump out the last of his extras. He repacked the empty bottles, zipped his bag, and struggled to reattach the pack to his back.

Kelly buried her head in her hands in frustration. Finally, she snatched the pack away from Hector. "I'll carry it."

"How about we all take turns?" Violet offered.

Kelly strapped the pack around her waist and stood tall. "I can handle it." She turned to Hector. "You need a granola bar or your teddy bear or whatever other ridiculous things you packed, just let me know, and we'll make a special stop for you."

Crimson anger rose in Hector's face as Kelly took the lead. Violet put her hand on his shoulder. "Hey. Deep cleansing breath. We're all friends here."

"Why did you bring her? She hates me!" he whispered.

"I can hear you, and we're wasting time," Kelly said from ten feet ahead. "Let's move."

Violet prodded Hector along. "I brought her because she's better at hiking and outdoorsy stuff than us. And she wants to get to the bottom of the whole Happy Harry thing, just like we do. Plus, she can beat up guys twice her size."

"And guys half my size too," Kelly called out.

"You're so funny," Hector snapped.

"And Kelly," Violet said, "Hector is actually really good at helping me figure stuff out, and he learns from his mistakes. So let's cut him a little slack. Maybe we can all just agree to get along and enjoy . . . looking into this terrifying situation."

Dead silence hung in the air. Kelly didn't even look back. Hector scowled at the ground as he walked.

"Okay, glad we cleared that up," Violet muttered.

"You guys have fifteen minutes at this stupid cemetery, and then we're turning around," Kelly finally said.

"I promise this will all be quick and painless," Violet said. "Kelly, thank you so much for coming. I owe you one."

"There probably won't even *be* a cemetery," Hector grumbled.

Kelly stopped and turned. "What makes you say that?"

"Violet asked me to look up cemeteries the other day, and I couldn't find the one on Gary's map. Not online."

Kelly glared at Violet now. "Are we seriously looking for something that might not even *exist*? Violet Black, I'm going to kill you!"

"Hector never told me that!" She hit him on the shoulder.

"Ow! You never asked! I forgot!"

"Well don't you think that might be important information?" Kelly snapped.

"You guys, come on." Violet got between them. "I'm sorry. I should have followed up with Hector. But truthfully, this could be good news."

Kelly marched onward. "Good news because we're not going to a creepy old cemetery?"

"Okay, *relatively* good news. It means that if there is a cemetery, it's probably a really old forgotten one. Something locals try to keep hidden. That supports our supernatural cover-up theory."

"I really doubt we're going to stumble upon a hidden cemetery," Kelly said.

"Why not?" Violet asked. "Graves are everywhere, whether we know it or not."

Kelly slowed down and allowed Violet to catch up. Her expression softened. "What do you mean?"

Violet positioned herself between Kelly and Hector. "I mean most cemeteries we know about are just the *recently* buried. Past hundred years or so. But the land we're standing on has been occupied by people since ancient times.

"Native Americans, settlers, and pioneers buried their dead for centuries using simple stone or wood markers that just washed away with time. Battlefields, plagues, and natural disasters devastated people by the hundreds, and the survivors had no choice but to bury the dead where they lay."

"So you're saying that everywhere we go is a graveyard?" Hector asked.

"Well, anywhere could *possibly* be a graveyard. Just because you're standing on a spot where a dead person was buried, doesn't mean something bad will happen. But sometimes if you disturb a grave--actually dig it up--that can lead to a haunting."

"How do you know about this?" Kelly asked.

"It's sort of the family business," Violet explained. "See my dad is a professor like I said. But he studies special situations."

"He's a ghost hunter!" Hector exclaimed.

"Ghost hunter makes it sound kind of hokey," Violet said. "Let's say paranormal investigator."

Kelly shook her head. "I don't believe in that stuff."

"I don't blame you," Violet said. "A lot of people don't. It's hard to believe. And some of the people who *claim* to believe it are wackos, uh, mentally ill. But the cases that my dad looks into . . . that my whole family used to check out . . . they always involved level-headed people. One day they experience something weird, and they have no idea why." Violet winked at Hector.

Hector smiled.

"Why though? Because they dug up some grave?" Kelly asked.

"Sometimes. Like last Christmas break, my dad got a tip from a colleague about this case outside Savannah, Georgia. Brand new housing development. First family to ever live in this house. Haunted to the roof."

"They built it on a grave," Hector said.

"Exactly. Construction crews disturbed the bones of two Civil War ghosts: a Union soldier and a Confederate. They had killed each other in a nearby swamp, and their remains had been swallowed up by nature. A century and a half later, they resumed their battle in some family's living room."

"How did you get rid of them?" Hector asked.

"We had to resolve their struggle. These two hated each other because of a war that was long over. Once we got through to them that it was the 21st century and the Civil War was over, they passed on."

"So how do we get rid of Happy Harry?" Hector asked.

Violet was hoping he wouldn't ask that. Quite frankly she didn't know. "Harry's different," she said. "That's why we need to learn more about him."

Kelly shook her head. "I still don't believe in ghosts."

"You don't have to," Violet said. "I hope neither one of you ever sees one again, to be honest. But let's not count on that."

The path wound westward, revealing the northern half of Lake Coldwater. A great blue heron swooped down and perched on the sandy shore. The surface of the lake shimmered in the sunlight, and the music of the loons echoed in the distance. Violet wished they had come for the scenery instead of the investigation.

"Okay." Kelly took a good look around. "Coldwater's a narrow lake. So if we keep going this way we're going to start rounding the other side." She faced the clearing to the north. "If there is a cemetery, it's going to be close by. I will help you look for fifteen minutes, but that's it."

"Sounds good," Violet said. She took the map out of her pocket and unfolded it for everyone to see. "We're looking in this general area. Gary jotted '12' down here. Not sure what that means. Twelve paces north? Twelve feet? Twelve graves?"

"Better not be twelve miles," Kelly muttered.

"It won't be," Violet said. "Don't wander too far. Look for unusually shaped stones in or on the ground. Okay. Let's split up, gang."

Hector and Kelly stared blankly.

"Sorry." Violet shrugged. "I always wanted to say that."

Kelly rolled her eyes and headed into the brush.

The field north of the lake teemed with tall dry grass and wildflowers. Violet brushed foliage away with her feet as she searched for markers. If there was an old cemetery, it was probably overgrown. *This might take longer than Kelly's fifteen minutes,* she thought.

"If I get a tick, I'm holding you accountable, Black!" Kelly called out.

"You're the best, Kelly!" she returned.

Violet scoured a thirty-square-foot area. She was afraid their fifteen minutes was just about up, when Hector called from the northeast, "Hey, Violet?"

"Yeah?"

"What kind of last name is Hellberg? Swedish, Danish, or Norwegian?"

Violet raced over to him and emerged in a wide section of short, green grass. Sure enough, in the middle of the clearing, Hector had discovered a well-kept area with flowers and five stone markers. Etched in each stone were names: Marta Hellberg, Christian Hellberg, Elisabeth Hellberg, Gonnar Hellberg. Bright blue flowers surrounded the most prominent marker, which read: "In Memory of Helen Hellberg. Loving Mother and Wife to Harald. 1892-1927."

"Jackpot," Violet whispered.

Kelly joined them. She knelt for close inspection and shook her head in disbelief. "Wife to Harald."

"Wife to *Harry*," Hector said.

"It's a family cemetery," Violet said. "That's why you couldn't find it online, Hec. What's even more amazing is that it's been recently tended." She pointed to the crackly tall grass that circled the clearing. "All that brush has been kept back. These flowers have been watered in the summer heat. Someone maintains this."

"Do you think it was Gary?" Hector asked.

"Well, we know he knows about this, at least," Violet said.

"Okay," Kelly said. "So there really was a Harald who lived by Lake Coldwater a long time ago, and his family is dead. But so what? People who lived a long time ago are dead. Campers probably found this graveyard and made up the story years ago."

"Maybe," Violet said. "But Helen died when she was only thirty-five. And the way this is set up leads me to believe these were all her kids. No dates on their graves. They probably died around the same time."

"So they made up a story to match the graves," Kelly insisted.

Hector shook his head. "Violet, there's no grave for Harry. You were right. He never died. So he's not a ghost. But what *is* he?"

Kelly groaned. "You guys are getting carried away. When you're done playing Scooby Doo, meet me on the trail, and we'll go home." Kelly struck off towards the lake and screamed in terror.

The old woman in the green cloak stood behind them. She scowled with her fists balled up, eyes wide, jaw shaking. "You stay away from this place!" she hissed. "Stay out of these woods! Go far away and never look back!"

She threw both arms in the air and tossed a cloud of white powder. Then with a flourish of her green cloak, she hobbled off through the grass.

"Oh my God!" Hector exclaimed. "It's anthrax! We're poisoned! We're going to die!"

Kelly had received the brunt of the strange powder. She stood dazed and wide-eyed; her hands shook.

Violet wiped Kelly's arm, then licked the tip of her finger. "It's salt."

"Why did a crazy lady just throw salt at me?" Kelly finally shouted.

"Because she's *not* crazy," Violet said. "We have to follow her!"

15

Violet raced to the main path. She spotted the old woman's green cloak rounding the west side of the lake.

Kelly dusted salty residue off her clothes as she caught up. "Whoa! Hold up, Violet! I've had enough crazy adventuring for one day. We're heading back."

"I have to talk to that lady." Violet raced down the path. The woman moved quickly for her apparent age.

"Why do you have to talk to a crazy lady?" Kelly implored.

"She's not crazy."

"Okay. Explain that part to me."

"That stuff she threw at us was salt-based. Salt purifies the air against demons. She was trying to protect us."

Kelly grabbed Violet's shoulders and spun her around. "No offense, but that actually sounds *really* crazy!"

"Crazy. Superstitious. Whatever you want to call it. She's not trying to hurt us. She thinks we're in danger. Remember what she said at the lake? She compared the campers to lambs for slaughter."

"That also sounds crazy," Kelly insisted.

"*She's* not out to slaughter us, but she knows who is."

Hector struggled to catch up, dragging his oversized pack. "Happy Harry?"

"All signs point to yes." Violet continued after the woman.

Kelly grabbed her wrist. "Violet, this is not a good idea."

Violet paused to consider, then nodded. "You're right."

"Thank God!" Kelly proclaimed.

"You guys should go back. If there are fewer people, she might not feel threatened." Violet continued her pursuit. "I'll let you know how it goes. Get back to camp. Cover for me if you have to."

"You are insane!" Kelly followed Violet once more. Hector grunted and struggled with the pack. Finally, Kelly shouted to him, "Give me that!"

Violet rounded the opposite side of the lake. The path continued straight, but the old woman had vanished. That meant she had probably ducked into the trees.

Kelly caught up to her, Hector's pack strapped over her shoulders. "Violet, I'm really mad at you. Let's go home."

Violet studied the west side of the trees as she walked. "Maybe there's an offshoot from the main path," she thought aloud. "Salt lady probably has no car, so she must live nearby."

"Are you even listening to me?" Kelly snapped.

Violet turned to Kelly. "I am. And I'm really sorry you're mad. You should take Hector back to camp. You can leave that pack with me; I'll carry it home and everything. You guys have done enough. Thanks."

"I'm not going back," Hector said. "I'm staying with Violet."

"You're both being stupid!" Kelly exclaimed. "That lady is nuts. She doesn't want to talk. And besides, if there really is a psycho stalking the woods with an ax, we need to *get back to camp*!"

"All valid points," Violet said. "But I remain determined." She finally spotted a small opening through the trees. She approached it and found a narrow, grassy path. "Inconspicuous, but maintained," she said. "Brilliant."

"If by brilliant, you mean a pathway to a nutty old bag who throws salt at kids," Kelly snapped.

Violet shrugged. "She might be a very charming, but eccentric, wise senior citizen."

"*Might* be. And we *might* be in a whole lot of trouble if we don't get back. We're not going in there." She folded her arms in refusal.

"Hey, Kelly," Hector said. "Either go home, or stop complaining."

Violet tried to hide her amusement.

Kelly bit her lip and shook her head in frustration. "If you guys are really this stupid . . . then you might need protection."

"That's the spirit," Violet said. "And if we do get in trouble, Hector and I promise to explain that you were the voice of reason, coerced to join us for our own good."

"Unless we get killed," Hector said. "Then you'll have some explaining to do."

"You're developing a dark sense of humor, Mr. Chang. I like that." Violet patted his back. "Comes in handy in this business."

Kelly glared.

They entered the shady path. Trees closed around them. They pushed through patches of thick brush. A jet black squirrel shuffled through a tuft of tall grass. It cocked its head at Violet and then darted off. The canopy thickened until only narrow beams of sun filtered through. Nailed to a wide oak were two wooden signs that read: "No Trespassing!" "Keep Away!"

"That's promising," Kelly said.

"You scared?" Hector said. A quick black object streaked down the path between Hector's legs. He screamed at the top of his lungs.

"Shh!" Violet covered his mouth. She pointed down the trail to a lithe black cat. "It's a kitty, Hector." The cat licked its paw and cleaned its forehead.

"Sorry," he whispered.

They continued. The path opened to a bright green clearing. A red cottage stood upon the far end. Its slanted roof teemed with moss and vines. A stone chimney jutted from the back end, and a pyramid of firewood had been stacked neatly against it. A gray brick well sat between them and the house.

"Wow." Violet stood in admiration. "That's a little more European countryside than I expected."

Violet spotted the old woman's face peeking from behind a blue checkered curtain in the window. She withdrew once Violet made eye contact. Moments later, the door swung open. "You're not welcome here! Get back to your camp and get away from this lake! Far away, before the Devil feasts upon your bones!" She slammed the door so hard that a log rolled off her stack of firewood.

"Okay," Kelly said. "I don't think she wants to talk, Violet. Good effort though. Let's go home."

Violet pondered aloud, "If I was a cranky old lady in the woods who hated everyone, how would I want to be approached?" The answer strutted across the clearing in the form of a slender orange-striped tabby. "She's a crazy cat lady!" Violet exclaimed.

"Is that better or worse than being a crazy lady who throws salt and talks about the Devil feasting upon our bones?" Kelly asked.

"Better!" Violet crossed the clearing to the front door and knocked.

"Go away!" the old woman screeched.

"We're sorry to bother you, ma'am," Violet explained. "But I couldn't help but admire the beautiful orange tabby. He's so majestic and confident. It's like he doesn't have a care in the world."

There was a long silence.

"We saw a handsome, healthy black cat on the path too," Violet added. "I think it's nice that you take care of all these animals."

Violet counted down in her head: *Three, two, one . . .*

"That was Twilight on the main path. The tabby is Ember," the woman said.

"That's beautiful. Like a warm, glowing fire," Violet gushed. Talking to people about their pets instantly put them at ease. Violet's mother had taught her that. She remembered an occasion in Paris when her father was going in circles with a snooty innkeeper. Her mother had stooped down, scratched behind the ears of the owner's yipping cocker spaniel, and suddenly they were all best friends.

The woman opened the door; her wrinkled face beamed. "Young lady, you really ought to go back. Phone your parents and tell them to take you away from this terrible place."

"I was hoping we could talk about that," Violet said. "If we know more about the danger we're in, maybe we can stop it."

The woman gazed over Violet's shoulder at Hector and Kelly. She lowered her voice, "I don't mean to frighten you. But there is no stopping this evil."

"If you didn't want to frighten us, you probably shouldn't have said the Devil was going to eat our bones," Kelly said.

The old woman's face flushed with embarrassment.

"I'm sure you were only trying to scare us so that we'd go home and be safe," Violet offered. "But actually, we've seen a few scary things already. And we'd be so grateful if you could help us understand them."

The woman took Violet's ankh charm between her bony fingers. Violet fought the urge to snatch it back.

The old woman rubbed the ankh. "There's positive energy in this item."

"My mother gave it to me." Violet's eyes misted. *This woman definitely has some kind of spiritual know-how.* "Could we please come in and talk?" Violet asked. "Just for a bit?"

The woman nodded. "Come in. Come in." She opened the door wide to reveal a single room with a modest bed, a few chairs, a stone fireplace, piles of books, boxes, and other odds and ends.

Violet entered. She motioned for Hector and Kelly to follow, but they remained hesitant. She mouthed, "Come on!" They cautiously made their way inside.

Landscape paintings of the lake during different seasons and all kinds of weather adorned the walls, along with crosses of various sizes, colors, and shapes. Above a kitchen nook, rows of different colored soils and powders lined the shelves.

"I don't have any food to offer, I'm afraid," the woman said. "It's been some time since I've had visitors."

"That's all right," Violet said. "These are my friends Hector and Kelly." They each gave a little wave. "I'm Violet."

"Oh my!" The woman chuckled with delight. "Like the color of your hair. You're like a flower."

Violet smiled. "That's right."

"My name is Anna. I've lived alongside this lake a long time."

"It's a beautiful place," Violet said. "The water, and the trees, and the wildlife."

Anna dismissed Violet with a wave of her hand. "Oh, it's a terrible place! It grows more terrible every year. Though beautiful, yes. Quite lovely."

Violet pointed to the different jars in the kitchen. "So you threw salt back at the gravesite."

She nodded. "Salt cleanses the air of bad energy."

"Yeah, I was just telling Kelly about that," Violet said.

Anna continued, "When a demon encounters a pile of salt, it must stop and count every grain, you know. Throw salt, and they will never catch up to you."

"Oh," Violet said. "Did you think that we were demons?"

"You never can be too sure in these woods!" She laughed.

"Violet," Kelly whispered under her breath, "let's get out of here."

"Why don't you children have a seat?" Anna pointed to four dusty stools around her table. "I'll fetch some water and see about boiling a pot of tea." Anna made her way to the door and disappeared.

Kelly grabbed Violet by the collar. "Let's get out of here, let's get out of here, let's get out of here!"

"I agree," Hector said. "That lady thinks we're demons. She wasn't trying to protect us; she wanted us to count salt."

"But now she knows we're human," Violet said. "Come on you guys. I'm getting a good vibe from her. Eccentric, but harmless."

"And what the heck is this? Rock soup?" Hector stooped over a metal basin full of frothy liquid. Violet leaned over it and saw that the bottom was full of flat white stones. Hector reached in.

"Don't touch that!" Anna shouted from the doorway. "Those stones must bathe in pure waters until the moon is full."

"Sorry," Hector said.

Anna clutched a wooden bucket. "I don't know that I have leaves for tea, so perhaps some hot water."

"I love hot water," Violet said. "Good for the throat."

Anna smiled and set up a kettle above her fireplace. She stooped and furiously rubbed two sticks together.

"Well Anna, I admire you for living independently out here," Violet said. "Hector here can't even leave camp without a computer."

Anna giggled. Smoke wafted from the friction of her kindling. "I don't even know about computers!"

Soon Anna sparked a small fire. She reached for an accordion-shaped fireplace bellows and fanned her little flame until it spread. Then she joined them at the table. "So," her expression grew dark, "you children have seen him?"

"Happy Harry?" Violet asked. "He attacked Hector, and then he appeared on the other side of the lake. Everyone at camp saw him."

Anna shook her head. "It's starting then."

"What's starting?" Hector asked.

"Harry's cycle," Anna said. "I've tried my best to keep him at bay over the years. During Harry's last rampage, my husband plunged a dagger of sacred stone into that foul demon's heart."

"Where is that dagger now?" Violet asked.

"Gone to ash . . . along with the brave man who wielded it."

"I'm sorry."

Anna sighed. "So am I. My James repelled him that time. He saved a lot of lives at the cost of his own. But Happy Harry *always* comes back. About every twenty years or so, he marks these woods with some dark, terrible deed."

"The cemetery. That's Harry's family?" Violet asked.

Anna sighed. "Yes. It's a sad story, isn't it?"

Violet nodded. "But you say you've lived here your whole life. What does Harry keep coming back for exactly?"

"Harry's murderous impulses wax and wane with the moon," Anna explained. "He lays dormant for decades at a time. But I knew the moment I saw them building that terrible camp. A place for *children!*" She spat. "Children!"

"Do you not like children?" Kelly asked.

"Oh, children are delightful." Her tone shifted. "Why I once had . . ." She stared off dreamily.

"I think I understand this," Violet said, interrupting the awkward silence. "Happy Harry stalked the paths before. For a long time, he would come and go."

Anna nodded. "In darkest night, he whistles his terrible song in hope that innocent blood will wander into his path."

"Except," Violet said. "Sometimes he goes away, for long stretches of time."

"Harry is restricted to the path. I've tried to keep it that way."

"But when they built the camp," Violet continued, "year after year, the woods were full of children. It brought him back somehow, didn't it? The teeming scores of innocent kids, laughing, playing, sleeping just out of reach every night. And the story came back too."

Anna nodded. "Bad energy simmers like a stew. When you fear a dark demonic spirit, they feed on that energy. The more you acknowledge it--"

"--the stronger it becomes," Violet finished.

"So what?" Hector said. "Do we have to get kids to stop telling the story? If we ignore Happy Harry, he can't hurt us?"

"I doubt it'll be that easy," Violet said. "Anna, we need another one of those stone daggers that your husband used. How did you--"

"Listen to me." Anna's eyes darkened. "*Nothing* can be done. You children *must* leave. Go far away. Certain events are in motion that cannot be stopped. Your presence makes things worse."

"So unless the kids go away, Harry will stick around," Violet said. "And he'll get stronger every year."

Anna nodded. "That's what I fear."

"How long has Camp Coldwater been here?" Violet asked. "Ten years? Why now? Why is Harry finally getting strong enough to show himself to the campers?"

The tea kettle gave a shrill whistle. Anna went to fetch it. Violet took another look around the cottage. *There's something she's not telling us,* Violet thought. *Or maybe even something she doesn't quite realize herself.*

Violet spotted an old photograph in a five-by-eight metal frame. She crossed the room and examined the image of a smiling freckle-faced boy who couldn't have been much older than ten. "Is this your son?" Violet asked.

Anna stopped pouring hot water into her mugs. She stared up, stone-faced. Steam from the boiling liquid wrapped around her.

"I'm sorry," Violet said. "I didn't mean to pry."

"Did Happy Harry . . . kill your son?" Hector asked.

Anna scowled.

"Hector," Violet said, "that's really not our business--"

Anna slammed her kettle down and pointed to the door. "You children get out of here. Get back to that wretched camp, telephone your parents, and leave this place forever."

"Anna, please." Violet returned to the table. "We don't have to talk about your son or even what happened to your husband. I just want to know about--"

Anna smashed a mug against the stone fireplace. She turned back to Violet and screamed. "Get out of here! Get out of here before the searing hot blade of the Devil finds your back!"

Hector and Kelly's eyes widened.

Anna screeched, "GET OUUUUUUUUUUUUUUT!"

Kelly and Hector bolted for the exit. Hector's oversized pack snagged on the door frame. He fumbled with it for a few seconds before it unlatched and sent him toppling outside.

Violet took a step towards the fireplace. "Anna, please--" Kelly returned, grabbed Violet's arm, and dragged her out.

Anna continued to shriek inside the cottage.

Violet wriggled her arm free from Kelly's grip. "Let go! She's not dangerous, just a little--"

Anna slammed the door. It echoed like thunder, and the pile of firewood collapsed. The orange tabby who had been sleeping nearby screeched and darted into the woods.

"Sensitive," Violet finished.

"Well!" Kelly snatched Hector's pack away from him. "That went well! Crazy woman is crazy! What exactly did you think you were going to learn in there, Violet?"

"We learned a lot actually," Violet said. "If you hadn't stopped me, I could have--"

"If I hadn't *dragged* you away, that old coot was probably going to splash scalding water in your face!" Kelly screamed. "I'm leaving! With or without you guys!" She stormed off down the narrow path, towards the lake.

After a long silence, Hector said, "She's mad."

Violet sighed and stared into the sky. Gray clouds drifted past the sun. She checked her watch: 2:20 p.m.

"Violet," Hector said. "I think Kelly's really mad at you."

"I heard you the first time, Hector."

"Sorry. You think she's going to tell on us?"

"No, I don't. But we should probably catch up to her. Safety in numbers." Violet headed towards the path. Hector followed.

"Plus, she has all the food," he added.

"That too."

She and Hector made their way back through the trees in silence. Loons sang in the distance. The black cat that had startled Hector meowed curiously as they passed.

"Violet?" Hector asked.

"Yeah?"

"What exactly *did* we learn from that crazy lady?"

Violet struggled, "I don't know. Lots of things. About Harry."

"Harry's bad. He wants to kill kids. I already knew that."

"Well, you shouldn't have asked about her son like that."

"*You* asked about her son," Hector said. "You picked up the picture. I was just trying to help."

"It was rude!" Violet snapped. "People whose families are killed by demons don't like to talk about it."

"But that's why we went in there."

"Well . . . you have to talk about it a certain way."

"All right, I'll just shut up next time," he muttered.

They reached the main path and trudged north around the lake in silence. Kelly was already well out of sight. Thunder rumbled in the distance.

"Great!" Hector mumbled. "It's gonna rain, and I don't have my poncho. Kelly took everything!"

"Quit complaining," Violet said. "Kelly's going to get your computer home in time to keep it dry. Be grateful."

As they rounded the lake, the sky darkened. A cold breeze blew across the water. The thunder grew louder. Treetops shook in the wind. "Next time we sneak out, Hector, please check the weather before we go."

"Sure blame the rain on me. Blame *everything* on me."

"That's not what I meant! You're so dramatic. Not everything's a personal--"

Hector stopped and held up his hand for silence.

"What?"

The wind howled.

"Hector, we have to keep moving."

"Shh!" The color drained from his face.

Then Violet heard it too: the faint, ghostly whistling of "Hall of the Mountain King."

16

Violet grabbed Hector's shoulders. "Can you run?"

He nodded.

"Not a good time to lie."

He shook his head. "Not very far. Not for long."

Violet's mind raced. *Hopefully, Kelly's far enough away by now. But is Harry north or south of us?* The wind whipped in circles. She couldn't tell which direction Harry's tune was coming from. *Either make our way around the lake and hope Harry's behind us, or head back to Anna's cottage.*

"Violet," Hector's voice trembled.

"I'm thinking, I'm thinking." Anna wouldn't be happy to see them, but she seemed to know a thing or two about purification, so Harry probably wouldn't be able to follow. "Back to Anna's house. Come on." She yanked Hector's arm southward.

"How come?"

"Because we--"

"Duck!" Hector pulled Violet backward as something wooshed overhead. A few strands of purple hair fluttered onto her chest. She stared up at the lanky figure of Happy Harry.

His eight smoldering eyes burned at her. His jagged pumpkin mouth flickered against his leathery face. His tattered coat flapped in the wind. He hoisted the gnarled handle of his ax. The crescent blade sliced down. Violet rolled away.

Shunk! The blade wedged into the earth. The smell of burned soil met Violet's nostrils. Harry struggled to free his ax from the ground.

Hector yanked Violet to her feet, and they ran. Thunder cracked. Rain splattered into a downpour. "Can you swim?" Violet shouted.

"A little!"

"Head for the lake! Some demons don't like to cross water!"

"Is he chasing us?"

"Don't look back, Hector; people never like what they see!"

Hector glanced back, then stopped in his tracks. "Look out!" He tackled Violet towards the forest. Harry lurched forward, slamming his blade into the path where Violet would have been. Harry's boots skidded in the mud. He yanked his weapon into the air once more. A raspy, otherworldly laugh echoed over the raindrops.

Lightning cut across the sky, followed by a ground shaking clap of thunder. Hector scrambled to his feet. "Come on!"

He's too fast, Violet thought. *We'll never outrun him.* She held up her hands. "Harry, listen to me."

"Oh please, Violet! Don't talk to him!" Hector said. "This is not the crazy old lady; this is a bad idea!"

Harry's laugh continued. He strolled towards them, ax slung over one shoulder.

"I know what happened," Violet's voice shook. "I know you made a deal, but you made another promise. To Helen."

"This is not going to work," Hector cried behind her. "Oh God, please just run with me."

Violet kept her arms in front of her. "You promised Helen you would take care of the children."

Harry stopped. He tilted his head like a lion considering its prey.

"Take care of Marta. And Christian." Violet continued, "Elisabeth and . . ."

"Gonnar," Hector whispered. "The last one was Gonnar."

"And Gonnar," Violet said. "Don't forget Gonnar. Remember their faces. Remember how much they loved you. Trusted you."

Harry lowered his ax. His smile flickered beneath his eight eyes.

"Killing us isn't going to make you happy because it never lasts. He tricked you, didn't he? The Devil tricked you, and you want this to end. Don't you?"

Harry's thumb rubbed the gnarled handle of his ax. Rain steamed against the hot blade.

"It's working," Hector whispered.

Violet saw his grip tense around the handle. The message on the fallen tree resurfaced in her mind. "I SAW YOU!" *No,* she realized, *he doesn't care. He's just toying with us.* "Run!"

She leapt backwards as Harry swiped his ax and laughed.

Violet scrambled to her feet and shoved Hector into the woods. They fought through the trees. Branches poked, and leaves whipped their faces. Water poured from the canopy. *Harry's bigger than us,* Violet thought. *And that ax can't be easy to maneuver through dense forest.*

Once they'd gained enough distance, she shoved Hector into the brush. He shouted and cried, but she pulled his head down and hushed him. "It's me. Be quiet. Stay low."

She got onto her elbows and observed the path. The glow of Harry's face danced between the tree trunks. *He's still on the trail,* she thought. *Just waiting.*

Lightning lit the forest in bright flashes. Thunder growled, and water trickled down in steady streams. *Nobody knows these woods better than Happy Harry,* she thought. *In a game of hide and seek, we'll lose.*

She whispered to Hector, "We have to split up. He can only chase one of us."

"Please don't leave me," Hector begged. "Let's just stay here. Right here until he goes away."

"He's not going away," Violet said.

Hector choked up. He shook his head.

"I'm scared too, okay. But there's one of him and two of us." She glanced up again. Harry continued to pace the trail. The wind died down for a moment, and "Hall of the Mountain King" echoed through the trees.

"Maybe he can't leave the trail," Hector whispered.

Violet shook her head. "But what if he *can*? He likes to play games. He knows we're here. He knows we can't stay here forever. He's watching and waiting."

Violet pointed north. "Crawl that way, Hector. As far as you can. Stay low. I'll crawl south. Then I'm going to stand up and make a lot of noise. When he comes into the trees to get me, make a break for the trail. Go north, around the lake, back to camp. If Harry follows you, go in the water and hope he can't swim."

"What about you?"

"The trees will slow him down, and I'll make it to Anna's cottage. Sound like a plan?"

Hector nodded.

Something sizzled right above them. They both glanced up to find Harry's terrible grin beaming down at them. Raindrops boiled down his searing hot ax and evaporated. He whistled a bar of his tune.

They leapt to their feet as he chopped into the brush. "North!" Violet screamed. She darted southward towards Anna's house.

Violet slipped in mud, stumbled, and scraped her knee on a patch of twigs. She swiftly returned to her feet and kept moving. *Please,* she thought, *please chase me and not Hector.* She knew in her heart that Hector could never outrun him. She dreaded that somehow Harry knew it too.

She dodged behind a thick oak and peered back cautiously. The lantern glow of Harry's face bobbed about thirty feet back. Streams of water trickled down everywhere. But in the distance she heard Hector screaming for help. Harry hadn't followed him.

She clutched her mother's ankh. *Thank you, Mom,* she thought. A cloud of steam puffed into the air as Harry's ax passed under a stream of rainwater. *Now I just have to save my own skin.*

Harry's whistling carried through the woods. Distant thunder rumbled. Violet had wondered if Harry only came at night. But everyone had seen him at dusk the other day. *Maybe it's whenever the sun is gone or obscured,* she thought. *If it's dark, Harry hunts.*

Harry turned away from her location, and Violet slipped silently through the trees towards the main path. She angled her way further south, periodically glancing back to check the firelight of Harry's distant face.

She had run so frantically that she wasn't sure if she'd overshot the narrow path to Anna's home. *Worst case scenario, find the dock on the other side of camp and signal for a boat,* she thought. Either that or take her own advice and try swimming across. But truthfully, Violet was a terrible swimmer. She'd never make it. She'd be better off finding the main road and looping back to Camp Coldwater, the way she'd arrived with her dad on day one.

She remembered how she'd treated her dad on the way up. Now here she was having the most terrifying moment of her young ghost hunting career. "Next time we talk, Dad," Violet whispered under her breath, "I'll have quite a tale."

Violet found the main trail. She looked back and pushed her sopping wet bangs aside. Harry's glow lingered to the north. He was still searching deep in the trees. *Time to make a break for it.*

She shot down the wide open trail. Water blew over the lake in gray sheets. Her wet shoes splashed. The further south she ran, the clearer it became that she had overshot Anna's house by quite a bit.

Harry was going to pursue. She could count on it. She just needed as much distance between them as possible.

A gray bridge appeared on the horizon. It stretched over a creek that emptied into the lake, almost thirty feet below. Violet reached it and stopped to rest on its wooden post. Her heart pounded as though it might explode at any moment. She took just a few short breaths before looking up to find Harry strolling at a leisurely pace on the horizon.

He's walking! She wanted to cry. *Even at my top speed, Harry can keep up with me just by walking.* Violet shook her head and muttered, "You smug jerk."

Violet raced across the bridge. She slipped on a pool of water and fell face-first. Her head cracked against a support beam. Her vision blurred. She tried to get up, but she couldn't focus. After a moment, the hazy image of Happy Harry loomed over her. He whistled through his fiery grin.

Violet stumbled to her feet and steadied herself. She wanted to run, but every muscle throbbed. Every scrape and cut stung. Her head pulsed with each step Harry took in her direction.

Violet didn't know what else to do, so she held her mother's ankh and screamed as loud as she could. "Help!" She shouted until her throat scratched in pain. "Somebody please help me! Please!"

Harry laughed, reared back, and swooped his ax.

With a surprise burst of adrenaline, Violet dove out of harm's way. Harry's ax split the guard rail of the bridge. Planks of wood caught fire and plummeted three stories into the creek below. The bridge sparked licks of yellow flame at the touch of the hot ax, but rain smothered them out.

Harry laughed. He raised his ax to take a second swipe. Violet had nothing left. She couldn't keep fighting.

As Harry's blade cut the air, a massive green shape bashed him from the side. Harry lost his balance. He reached for the missing guard rail, stumbled, and fell.

Kelly stood upon the center of the bridge. She clutched Hector's oversized backpack like a medieval mace. "Where's a salt-throwing old lady when you need one?"

"Kelly!" Violet struggled to her feet and collapsed into a hug. "Oh my God, Kelly! I love you!"

"You okay?" She hugged her back.

"I am now. I've never been happier to see anyone in my entire life."

"I'm sorry that I didn't believe you," she said.

"Who cares! It's just that . . ." Violet let go of Kelly and rushed to the edge. She hadn't heard a splash. Harry was nowhere to be seen.

"What happened to him?" Kelly searched with her. "Did he get swept downstream?"

"I don't know." Violet examined the sky. The rain was letting up. Light beamed through thin gray clouds. "Maybe the sun came out."

17

Hector held the halves of his fractured netbook in each hand. "This is not happening." His eyes drooped in despair.

"I'm really sorry, Hector," Violet said. "I promise to save up and buy you a much better computer at the end of the summer."

"My baby." He lowered his head.

"Your baby took out Happy Harry." Kelly dropped Hector's sopping wet pack on the floor of the girls' cabin. It tipped over, spilling the remainder of its supplies. "We owe you one. Thanks for not packing light."

Hector gave a solemn nod.

"Hey, the rain probably would have ruined it anyway, bud. Think of it that way." Violet forced a smile.

"My dad's gonna kill me. I wasn't supposed to even bring it."

"Violet almost *did* get killed out there, so stop caring about your stupid computer." Kelly dried her hair and face with a towel from the bathroom. They were all soaked. Hector couldn't have beaten them back by much time. They had found him heading for the office to get help.

"Do you think anyone noticed we were gone?" Violet wrung water out of the lower half of her shirt.

"Doubt it," Kelly said. "Afternoon activities probably got rained out. I'll bet they're all in the cafeteria playing bingo or something."

The door of the girls' cabin swung open. Ronny flew in, red-faced and sniffling. She stopped in embarrassment, groaned, and left just as dramatically as she'd entered.

"Was she crying?" Hector asked.

Kelly and Violet exchanged curious glances. "You know, Hector, maybe you should go change into dry clothes," Violet said. "We'll find you later."

"Yeah." Hector set the pieces of his broken netbook back in his damp pack. He hoisted his supplies with a grunt and carried them out the front door.

"Wonder what's eating Ronny?" Kelly said.

"Good question. Wanna go find her?"

"I want to take a hot shower while there's no Becky to hog the bathroom."

"Cool. I'll be back." Outside, Violet heard soft sobs nearby. She found Ronny curled up against the side of the cabin.

"Hey, Ronny? Everything okay?"

"Leave me alone!"

"I know we're not friends or anything, but if there's a problem, I could go get a counselor or something."

"I hate these counselors! None of them care." She wiped her eyes.

"I hear ya," Violet said. "Sassy could out-sour a lemon. And Gary's kind of a phony."

"*Becky's* a phony!" Ronny sobbed.

Violet sat. "You and Becky have a fight?"

Ronny shook her head. "No. She's just a rotten, nasty brat."

"Well, I won't argue with that," Violet said. "But I thought you guys were friends."

"So did I."

"What did she do?"

"Whatever, it's none of your business. You don't like me. Why are you even talking to me?"

Violet shrugged. "Not sure. You haven't exactly been pleasant to room with so far."

"Then go away."

"What could Becky have done that was so bad, Ronny? I mean, she's been calling me a loser and a weirdo since I got here, and *I'm* doing just fine."

"Good for you," Ronny snapped. "If one of your stupid friends stabbed you in the back, you wouldn't like it."

"Good point," Violet said.

"Are you going to tell everyone that I cried?"

"Not really my style. It's actually refreshing to see your vulnerable side."

Ronny cracked a half smile.

"What did Becky say that was so bad? Come on. I won't tell anyone. Not even Kelly."

"We were playing this stupid game in the cafeteria. This dumb guessing game."

"Since it was raining outside?"

Ronny nodded. "And Becky says there's someone in the room with a . . . pointy witch nose and . . ." she gestured from her face down the length of her body, "bird legs, and a big rat's nest for hair, and . . ." She broke down again.

"What a jerk. Ronny you are really pretty. Especially when you smile nice like you just did a minute ago. Really pretty."

"No, I'm not. I'm a gawky, ugly girl. Becky only hangs out with me to make herself look better."

"Did she actually say that?"

"No. I just know it's true." She sniffled. "We've been friends since first grade, and she doesn't even care about me."

"Becky's just immature. You're very pretty. I wish I had full hair like yours. I wouldn't have to give myself purple highlights to try to look interesting."

Ronny smiled. "The highlights are cute . . . in a weird sort of punky way. I could see how like, a really weird guy would like it."

Violet laughed. "Wow. That was so close to *almost* being a compliment."

They both laughed.

Ronny shook her head. "I wish I could go home. I can't believe we haven't even been here a week. I just want to talk to my mom."

"You should call her. Actually, let me change into some dry clothes, and I'll go to the office with you. I wouldn't mind hearing my dad's voice right now."

Ronny gave her a funny look. "Um, we can't. Kids have been complaining since Gary made the announcement."

"Announcement?"

"Where have you been?"

Oh nowhere in particular, Ronny, just out in the woods getting hunted by an ax-wielding maniac. Violet shrugged. "I've been kinda spacing out today. What was the announcement?"

"He just told us like an hour ago. The storm knocked down a cell tower and blew out the phone lines. No reception, no landline."

"Oh." Violet's heart sank. *Happy Harry on the loose. Wild woman in the forest telling us to evacuate camp. And now there's no way for kids to even try to reason with their parents to come get them.* "Well, I'm sure they'll fix it soon."

"I hope so." Ronny rested her head against the cabin.

Violet stood. "I might take a walk, actually. But I hope you feel better."

"Thanks," Ronny said. "You're cool, Violet."

"I try." Violet smiled. "See ya."

After changing into dry clothes, Violet made her way towards the office. She wanted to hear about this phone blackout straight from Gary's mouth. Now that the rain had stopped, kids were starting to make their way outside from the cafeteria. But something didn't feel right.

Two girls bickered by the south cabins. A gang of amused spectators watched as one boy wrestled another to the ground in a headlock. Two of the Tucker Triplets carried an unfortunate kid upside down in a plastic garbage can towards the lake.

Everywhere Violet looked, kids were screaming, shouting, crying, or making trouble. And nowhere was there a single counselor doing anything about it. *Okay,* she thought. *Counselor apathy was bad before, but this is anarchy.*

A small girl ran screaming past her, pursued by a cloaked, ghost-masked Tucker Triplet. Violet stuck her leg out and tripped him. The Tucker flipped mask-first into the grass. Violet placed her wet shoe on the back of his head, pinning it down. Muddy water squished over his hood. "You'd better not be Brant," she said.

"I *am* Brant," he mumbled.

"I take it that means you're Brent, trying to blame Brant for this?"

An incriminating silence followed. She removed her foot, and he rolled onto his back. She unmasked him to reveal his flush, pudgy face. "Brent. Do you think it's appropriate to run around in scary costumes when half the kids are convinced that Happy Harry is going to chop them to pieces?"

Brent spit to one side then scowled. "That's the whole point, Clown-Hair."

"The whole point of what?"

"Why would I tell y--"

"The whole point," Violet stomped his cloaked gut, "of *what?*"

He groaned.

"Tell me what's going on with you and your brothers, or I'll stomp you so hard your stomach will be wedged between your lungs."

"Happy Harry . . ." he groaned.

"What *about* Happy Harry?"

"He doesn't kill the bad kids."

"Stop using that story as an excuse to pick on people."

"It used to be an excuse, but it's not anymore! We have to raise the stakes!"

Violet leaned closer. "What are you talking about?"

"He told him!"

"*Who* told *who?*"

"Happy Harry talks to Trent."

Violet's eyes widened. She took her foot away from Brent's belly. "What does Harry tell Trent to do? How does he talk to him? When does this happen?"

"I don't know. He only talks to Trent."

"I see." Violet crossed her arms. She watched as Trent and Brant tossed some poor kid, trashcan and all, into the shallow end of the lake. "I think I'm going to have a little talk with your boss."

18

Violet, Hector, and Kelly stared dumbfounded at the schedule posted in the office lobby. Beside every cabin number at every time of day was the word "OPEN!" Open schedules for every camper from breakfast through dinner all day long. Open. Open. Open.

Kelly shook her head. "A whole day of kids just hanging out, doing whatever they want, on nobody's time but their own?"

"Actually, when you put it that way, it sounds awesome," Hector said.

"It sounds weird." Violet eyed Gary's closed office door. "No phones. No contact with our parents. Half the counselors seem to be MIA, and suddenly nobody's even bothering to put together a schedule?"

"Maybe there was a walkout?" Hector suggested.

"What do you mean?" Kelly asked.

"An employee walkout. What if Gary did something to make the counselors mad, and they all quit?"

"Which means they don't have enough staff to run a normal day of activities." Violet pondered it. "That's almost too rational an explanation, considering the big weird picture."

Gary and Sassy emerged from his office. Gary gave Violet a funny look, then muttered something under his breath.

"Hey Gary!" Violet called out. "Phones back up yet?"

"Might be a while." He frowned. "I know you kids want to call your parents and let everyone know how much fun you're having, but bear with us."

"I was having trouble finding a counselor out there," Violet said. "A lot of kids are roughhousing. I think we need some adults."

"Sassy's a counselor. You found her." Gary forced a wide-eyed smile. "Dinner's in the cafeteria tonight. Too wet for a barbeque."

Gary headed outside. Sassy sighed. "Violet, Kelly . . ." She struggled for Hector's name. "Other kid. I'm really busy right now. Unless it's an emergency, you'll just have to fend for yourselves. Understood?" Sassy's tone lacked its usual snark. Something was off.

Violet nodded. "No problem. But if you guys can keep an eye on the Tucker Triplets, that'd be nice."

"Fine." Sassy followed Gary outside leaving the three of them alone in the lobby.

After a moment, Violet made a beeline for the open office door. "Cover me."

"Violet, don't go in there." Kelly sighed. "Hector, tell her to chill out."

Hector followed Violet. "This time you cover us, Kelly. I'm not making an idiot of myself again."

"You *guys*!" Kelly whispered as she followed.

The first thing Violet did was put Gary's phone to her ear. "No dial tone. You guys know any kids with a cell?"

"They're not allowed," Kelly said. "Kids abused them last summer."

Violet groaned. "Someone must have snuck one in, though. I want to know for sure if there's no signal." She started to search through Gary's drawers.

"What are you looking for?" Kelly asked.

Violet slammed a desk drawer. "I don't know. Something to help explain what's going on. If the counselors are quitting, or why they're quitting, or . . . something."

Kelly paced to the door and scanned the lobby. "We're gonna get caught."

"Not if we're fast," Violet said. "Come on guys, help. Look around. When Gary sees that the camp grounds have turned into a mud-encrusted insane asylum, hopefully it'll keep him distracted."

Kelly pointed to Gary's desktop calendar. "There's a big circle on today's date. That could mean something."

Violet examined the circle, but nothing was written inside it. "That could be anything." Violet activated the monitor on Gary's computer. A password screen popped up.

"Hector, what was Gary's email password?"

"Fortyfive45. Words then numbers, no hyphens. No case sensitive," he recited as he explored the wastebasket.

"Didn't work," Violet said.

"Fortysix46. He changes it and counts up."

She tried again, and the screen changed to a desktop background of Lake Coldwater. "Jackpot." Violet cracked her fingers in satisfaction. She clicked the internet icon, and an error message popped up. "Camp's offline," she said. "Storm must have knocked that out too." She opened Gary's documents, but there didn't seem to be anything interesting: flyers, rules and regulations, applications.

Violet opened a sub-folder labeled "disciplinary reports." She scrolled down the list. Not surprisingly, a huge portion of the alphabetized file names started with "Tucker."

"Some of these write-ups go back four years," Violet said. "I guess they're not kidding when they talk about permanent records."

She backtracked, clicked on another icon, and opened a spreadsheet of campers' names.

"Violet, we really should go," Kelly whispered.

"What's that, the room assignments?" Hector leaned over her shoulder. "Maybe we can edit me into a different room."

Violet gasped. "Hector, you genius!"

"What?"

She searched Hector's name. Cabin 12. His roommates: Nolan Wilson, Ziad Kearns, and Abel Addison.

"Hey, wait," Hector said. "That's not right."

Violet searched Kelly Powers, and she was assigned to a different cabin as well. No Becky. No Ronny.

"This spreadsheet is only a few weeks old," Violet shook her head. "These were the original room assignments." She scrolled down to the bottom of the document. "Approved by Michael Heart, Head Counselor of Camp Coldwater." She double checked the date again. Same summer, same year, long after the enrollment period had ended. Mere weeks before their session had started. "Who is Michael Heart?"

"Mike!" Kelly said. "He was head counselor last summer and the summer before. He taught me to tie a slipknot. He was *supposed* to help me with my archery this year."

"I remember Mike," Hector said. "Nice guy."

Violet closed the spreadsheet and clicked on another that was dated just days later. This one had Gary's name. "Looks like Mike *was* going to be head counselor this summer too, until Gary somehow got his job and mucked up his cabin assignments."

"Why would he do that?"

"I don't know." She returned to the documents folder.

"There!" Hector pointed at the screen. "Staff schedule. There's two in a row. Gary was taking Mike's files and just updating them."

Violet clicked on the slightly older staff schedule. A list of employees and assigned activities appeared.

"Hey!" Kelly peered closer. "Angie was supposed to stay on this summer. I loved Angie!"

"You guys recognize any other names?" Violet asked.

"Yeah, a few. Ethan McCallister . . . Lisa Garrett. I just assumed all these people moved on and got real jobs or went to college or something." Kelly huffed. "Why did Gary fire all the cool counselors?"

"When a new manager comes in, they like to bring in their own people sometimes," Hector said. "That's how my mom lost her job a few years back."

"Except all the new counselors are a bunch of stiffs," Kelly said. "They don't talk to you. They're no fun, they--"

"That's it!" Violet said.

"*What's* it?" Kelly asked.

"We should get out of here. Hector, if I turn off the monitor will that put Gary's password protection back on?" She closed out all the folders and put Gary's computer desktop back the way she'd found it.

"Just leaving it alone for a while should put it into sleep mode," Hector said.

"Good." She stood. "Let's go."

"Wait, though, what is all this about?" Kelly followed.

"I'll explain once we're away from--"

Gary glared at them outside his office. Keys jingled in his hand.

"Gary!" Violet's heart pounded. "I was seeing if you had internet . . . because I couldn't call my dad."

"My office is off limits." He scowled.

"I wanted to send my dad an email," Violet said meekly. "Hector was helping, but I guess there's a password or something."

"You kids are getting into everything," Gary hissed under his breath.

"You're right," Violet said. "Sorry. Kelly only followed us in to yell at us."

"Why is it," he leaned down until his eyes were just inches from her own, "that every time there's some kind of disturbance, I find you," he gestured towards Hector, "and your little friend?"

"We have names," Hector muttered.

"I realize you kids are upset that the phones are down. But being in my office is a bad idea. Very bad. Am I clear?" Gary's words hung like icicles.

"Crystal," Violet said.

"Good." He entered his office and slammed the door.

"Wow," Kelly said, once they had exited the lobby. "I didn't know that man could do anger."

Violet whispered, "He might be capable of worse."

19

The cafeteria was twice as rowdy as usual at dinner that night. Only two counselors remained stationed at either door. All the food put out had been cold or prepackaged. When Violet asked why, a sullen counselor merely said, "Kitchen staff is off tonight."

Back at the table, Violet picked at a chocolate muffin. "So why exactly does Gary fire all the fun counselors, hire surly ones, then bend over backward to rearrange the room assignments so that nice kids--like Hector Chang, Violet Black, and Kelly

Powers--are paired with mean kids like the Tuckers and Becky?" Violet asked.

"Why?" Kelly and Hector asked simultaneously.

"So that kids would be sure to have a miserable time."

"Not exactly a trick question," Kelly said. "But *why* would he want kids to have a bad time?"

Violet shook her head. "I don't know *exactly*. But Gary gathered records of troublemakers from past years. He went out of his way to schedule a crummy summer. And it's getting worse, isn't it? Tomorrow there are no activities planned. The mean kids are getting meaner, and the nice kids are getting--"

"Trampled," Hector said.

"Good word," Violet said. "I was gonna say overwhelmed, though."

"Oops!" Trent Tucker shoved Hector's chair as he walked by. Hector tensed and squirted his juice box in his own face. The Tucker Triplets snorted with laugher and continued on their way.

"Okay. Trampled." Violet handed Hector a stack of napkins. She watched the Tuckers systematically shove the chairs of other innocent diners as they made their way to their table. The pale twenty-something counselor picked his nose and watched indifferently from the door.

The Tuckers are part of this, Violet thought. *I'd better figure out what that means if Hector's sleeping under their roof.*

Hector slumped. "God, I hate them."

"I don't blame you," Violet said. "But we need to prioritize. I've got a job for you, Hector. Take a walk around the office buildings and check the phone and power lines. See if anything's been cut or fiddled with."

"I'm not an electrician." He shrugged. "I wouldn't know where to look."

"You're more technical than us. Take five. Wash up in the bathroom, and just give it a try."

He nodded, grabbed his tray, and headed away.

"You think he's gonna find anything?" Kelly unpeeled a banana.

"Maybe. Truthfully, that's not the priority." She lowered her voice, "The Tuckers are."

Kelly raised an eyebrow. "I don't follow. Gary's the one who--"

"Before I met up with you guys, Brent Tucker said something about how Trent talked to Happy Harry. He said Harry was telling them to pick on kids."

"They say that every year," Kelly said. "It's okay to be a bully because it means Harry won't get you." She bit her banana.

"What if it's true?" Violet said.

Kelly stopped chewing.

"Harry's real," Violet said. "The story seems to be real. He *really* delights in hunting and killing. You can see it in all *eight* of his eyes."

"Harry fell," Kelly said doubtfully. "Hopefully that's the end of him."

"It won't be. And it's getting dark out there already. I want to get to the bottom of this Trent Tucker thing. If Happy Harry is talking to him, when he's asleep or awake or whenever, I need to know more."

"So you sent Hector off, so he wouldn't have to get involved. Violet Black, you're the big sister he never had."

"I just don't want to make things worse for him," Violet said. "But I'll need some muscle on this."

Kelly smiled. "I eat Tuckers for breakfast."

After dinner, Violet and Kelly waited outside the cafeteria for the Tucker Triplets to exit. The three hulking boys emerged single file. They chortled like apes and headed towards the lake. Violet motioned for Kelly to wait until they had enough distance, then they followed.

"How do we know which one's Trent?" Violet asked.

"Trent's the one with the biggest mouth," Kelly whispered.

The Tuckers turned right at the shore and slipped into the trees.

Violet and Kelly approached cautiously. The Tuckers' laughter echoed through the shadows. Violet led Kelly off the main trail. She stepped carefully around sticks and leaves. Kelly tugged her sleeve and pointed. Glowing orange dots floated through the branches in front of them, about thirty feet away.

Cigarettes. The Tuckers had snuck out to smoke. *Should we try to listen in on their conversation?* Violet pondered. *Or do I just lay on the old Black family charm and talk my way into some info?* Violet motioned for Kelly to be still. She listened closely.

"So then this one dude was all DOOSH! And Brant's like WHAM! And the other dude goes running!"

The three of them laughed idiotically for what had to be a full minute straight.

"But that chick was screaming all crazy and stuff."

"Oh yeah, that chick was crazy!"

They laughed for more than another full minute.

Kelly's eyes rolled so far back into her head that she looked like she was going to pass out.

"And I was like WHAM!"

They laughed again, like a pack of monstrous hyenas.

Something, Violet thought. *Talk about something interesting, useful, relevant, please.*

"Hey Brent, what did that one dude go?"

Brent made a long, drawn-out explosion sound effect, and the three of them busted into laughter.

"Okay! I can't take this anymore!" Violet shouted.

The three shadowy masses turned in their direction.

Violet strolled out to meet them. "I hate to interrupt this scintillating repartee, but I'd like a word with Mr. Trent Tucker. Who would be . . ." She gestured with open arms at the three of them.

"Trent's the hot one," the middle Tucker said.

"I take it that's you," Violet said.

Trent took a long drag of his cigarette. He blew smoke in Violet's face. Kelly lurched forward, but Violet held up her arm. "No, Kelly, it's cool. Let's give these guys a chance."

Brent and Brant exchanged nervous glances on either side of their brother. Trent smirked. "Do you really think you could take me, Powers? You think you and your pale, weirdo gal-pal are going to threaten the three toughest kids--nay toughest *men* at this camp? Dream on."

"She doesn't have to, Trent," Violet said. "Personally, I don't care if you like polluting your lungs, but if you hurt us, we'll make sure Gary hears about you savoring cancer sticks on camp grounds."

Trent took another drag. "Do you seriously think these counselors care what we do? We've been getting away with *murder* all week."

"Not literally, though," Violet said apprehensively. "Right?"

"Huh?" Trent made a confused face.

"She means you're not really killing people," Kelly explained. "You're just being thugs."

"Well yeah, durh!" Trent scoffed. "We don't want to go to jail or nothin'."

"Okay, look," Violet explained. "You guys can smoke, or steal, or pick on kids to your hearts' content. At this point, I don't care. Bigger problems out there." She pointed down the trail. "So let's all just stay out of each other's way."

Trent groaned in frustration. "Then what are you doing here--"

Violet held up her hand. "I want to have a five minute conversation with you," she poked Trent in the chest, "about your dealings with a certain black-coated, ax-wielding, classical-music-whistling maniac who is something of a mutual acquaintance."

Trent's face softened. He stared Violet in the eyes. Violet smiled and nodded.

Trent took another puff of his cigarette. "Minute alone, boys."

"How come?" Brent and Brant whined simultaneously.

Trent gestured back to camp with his thumb. "Beat it!"

Brent and Brant each tossed the stubs of their smokes on the forest floor and stomped them out. They gave Violet and Kelly a pair of nasty glares and shouldered their way through the trees.

Trent waited until his brothers were out of earshot. "He made a deal with you too?"

"So you know he's real?" Kelly said. "You actually talk to him?"

"Know he's real?" Trent grew perplexed. "Of course he's real. He told me at the beginning of camp that me and my brothers were an important part of his plan and that . . ." Trent whispered, "That we couldn't tell anyone."

"Well, we already know," Violet said. "Go on."

"He said if we picked on kids, caused trouble, and generally ruined people's day that we were doing our jobs."

"Did you really see him?" Violet said. "Did you talk to him? Was it in your dreams?" Violet found it hard to believe that Happy Harry would come face-to-face with even a Tucker kid and not take a swing at him.

"What the heck are you talking about?" Trent shook his head.

"Happy Harry," Kelly said. "Happy Harry told you to pick on kids, and in exchange, he spares you, right? He takes out the weak ones and leaves the bad kids."

Trent stared back and forth between them in disbelief, then he broke into side-splitting laughter. "Oh man! That is the stupidest thing I ever heard! Oh, that's priceless! You guys are idiots! You believe in that garbage?"

Violet and Kelly exchanged lost expressions.

Trent continued to laugh so hard he was having trouble catching his breath.

"Okay, Tucker. This is all very funny," Violet said. "But truthfully, there *is* a Happy Harry. The whole camp saw him across the lake. Kelly and I saw him earlier today when it stormed. It's real."

"You guys are so gullible!" Trent managed to say through deep chortles. He suffered another fit of giggling punctuated by a long, piggish snort.

"You *just* got done saying you made a deal with someone," Violet said. "Your goon brothers *both* said something about you making a deal with Happy Harry. Both of them!"

Trent caught his breath. "Aw! They're just a couple of chumps! They're as gullible as anyone else."

"So who did you make a deal with? What's the deal!" Violet snapped.

"I'm not telling you; you guys don't know anything."

"You'd better tell us," Violet yelled. "Because a camp with no rules, no phones, no internet, and weird backdoor deals is bad news for all of us!"

Trent stopped smiling. "What do you mean?"

"She means that if you don't help us someone could be hurt," Kelly said. "Or killed. And it might be one of your brothers."

Trent stared into the trees for a moment. Violet could almost hear the rusty wheels turning in his head. Finally, he looked up and said, "Gary paid me."

"Gary? He paid you . . . money?" Violet asked.

"Yeah. He said it was for me and my brothers to cause trouble. He's been giving us each fifty bucks a day just to be troublemakers."

Violet nodded. "And you told your brothers the deal was with Happy Harry, so you could pocket their cut."

Trent smirked.

"Good brother," Kelly said. "Did it ever occur to you that it was really weird that a camp counselor was paying kids to be bad?"

Trent shrugged. "It was easy money. Win, win."

"It's odd, Trent. Why would a camp counselor want kids to be bad?" Violet turned to Kelly. "I was right. Gary's got some weird connection to Harry. The room rearrangements were to make kids more miserable, and he even bribed mean kids to be meaner." She turned back to Trent. "Do you know any other kids who Gary paid?"

"No," he said.

"Anything else we should know about?" Kelly pushed.

Trent shook his head.

"Thank you, Mr. Tucker," Violet said. "You've been most informative." Violet and Kelly turned back towards camp. Trent followed.

"Hey, don't tell my brothers what I did, okay?"

"That's the least of your problems," Violet said. "I suggest you get indoors. It's already pretty dark, and there are worse things than you and your idiot brothers in the woods."

Trent said nothing. He broke off in the direction of the lake. Violet and Kelly headed back to their own cabin. "We should find Hector and make sure he's okay," Violet said as they entered the door.

Ronny sat on her bed reading a book, but Becky was nowhere in sight. Violet headed to Becky's dresser drawer.

"What are we supposed to do if Gary . . ." Kelly trailed off as Violet opened Becky's drawer and sifted through her clothes. "Violet?"

Violet ignored her. *If this puzzle is coming together the way I think it is, then there should be some evidence in here.* Violet tossed a pair of Becky's jeans over her shoulder.

"Um," Ronny stood up. "What are you doing?"

Violet found what she was looking for: a roll of fifty dollar bills. She held it up. "Hey Ronny, you know how Becky's been even more of a monster than usual this summer? It's because Gary *paid* her to be mean." She tossed the money on the floor.

Becky emerged from the bathroom. She stared at the open drawer and the money on the floor. She fumed at Violet. "Why are you freaks going through my stuff!"

"Becky, I'd like to cut to the chase," Violet said. "I know you're just a confused girl who likes money and being mean. But why the heck was Gary paying you to pick on kids, including your own friend?"

Becky's mouth dropped. "I don't . . ." She stared at Ronny. "How did you know about . . ." She grimaced then shouted, "That money's from my dad!"

"Okay. You're no help at all!" Violet snapped. "That's fine. I don't expect stupid, spoiled brats to save themselves. I'll just have to do it myself. Come on, Kelly!"

Violet headed towards the cabin door just as an enormous blade hacked right through it. Wood charred against hot metal.

2◊

All four girls screamed as Happy Harry's ax pulled away and hacked again. Cinders sprayed into the cabin.

"Everybody out!" Violet pointed to the back window.

Ronny leapt to her feet and struggled with the window frame. "It doesn't open all the way!"

"Step aside." Kelly grabbed a baseball bat from under her bed. She bashed through the glass and swiped at the sharp edges along the bottom. "Careful going through."

Kelly helped Ronny over. Becky curled against the bed frame and shrieked hysterically. Harry's ax struck again, making a triangular hole in the door. He stuck his glowing, eight-eyed face through and laughed.

Kelly and Violet each grabbed one of Becky's arms and forced her to the window. Becky's eyes remained fixed on the door. Her screams rang in Violet's ear. Ronny reached for her from the other side, and the three girls managed to get her out. Harry's ax struck one last time, sending the entire door flying off its hinges.

"Get out!" Violet ordered. She attempted to take Kelly's bat.

"No!" Kelly tugged at her weapon. "I'll hold him off. *You* get out!"

Harry chopped through the middle of the bat. Both girls flew against opposite bunk beds. He stared between them, as if deciding which kill would be sweeter.

Something clocked Harry in the back of the head. He stumbled forward. Another whack from behind and Harry tripped into the open window. His ax stuck in the wall, and a sliver of blue flame ignited along the lodged blade.

"Come on!" Hector's white knuckles clutched a canoe paddle for dear life. He bashed Harry once more in the back. Violet and Kelly grabbed Hector and rushed out the front.

"I thought he could only attack us in the woods!" Hector shouted.

"Either we were wrong or something's changed," Violet panted. They neared the lake and stopped to catch their breath. Groups of kids had gathered around the dark fire pits. Violet almost shouted to them to run for the cafeteria or the office, but Gary was probably there. Unless Gary actually *was* Harry somehow. It was still possible. Either way, she wasn't quite sure where would be safe.

In the distance, smoke billowed from cabin 28. Orange light flickered in the windows. Harry emerged from the ruined doorframe as fire spread behind him. He tossed his ax over one shoulder and marched in their direction.

"He's specifically coming after us," Violet said. "He remembers us."

"That's bad," Hector said.

"That's good," Violet said. "It means that if we keep him busy he won't go after the other kids." Cabin 28 burned, but the surrounding cabins were spaced far enough apart to not catch fire. She shouted to the nearby campers. "Get to the cabins on the far side of camp!"

They stared in dumbstruck ignorance.

Kelly pointed. "That there is an ax murderer! Get out of here!"

Once the first kid screamed, the others scattered towards the office.

"Maybe they'll get help," Hector said.

"From who?" Violet wracked her brain for a plan. The eerie melody of "Hall of the Mountain King" drifted across the clearing.

"He thinks he's so bad taking his time to get us." Kelly took the canoe paddle from Hector. She raced to the dock. "Come on! Help me!" Kelly started to untie a canoe. Violet grabbed a second paddle. Once Kelly released the boat from its mooring, the three of them climbed inside. The canoe wobbled in the dark water, but it supported their combined weight. Kelly sat in back. "Violet, you're in front."

Violet protested, "But I'm not the best--"

"I'm worse," Hector insisted.

"He's right, Black. You're up!" Kelly ordered.

Violet couldn't argue as Harry's glowing grin bobbed through the picnic area. He spun his ax and diced through tables and benches. Flaming wood flew into the air.

"Show off," Violet muttered. She pushed the canoe away from the dock and paddled as hard as she could while focusing on Kelly's instructions.

"Straight, clean, fast strokes, Black! Come on! Beeline! Right through the water!"

Hector huddled between them on the floor of the canoe. His extra weight slowed them. Still, they made steady progress. *Keep it up,* Violet thought, her arms straining. *We're probably a good forty feet from shore by now.*

"Hey, Violet," Hector said.

"Yeah?" she grunted.

"Remember your theory that Happy Harry doesn't like to swim?"

"Uh huh."

"Well, you're wrong."

Violet glanced back for just a moment. Harry stood chest deep in the lake. His glowing face reflected in the rippling surface as he advanced. "Good to know, Hector. Thank you."

Stop looking back, she told herself. *It never pays to look back. Strong, straight strokes, one at a time. Listen to Kelly.* Soon they were halfway across the lake. Her arms burned in exhaustion.

"Can you see Harry, Hector?" Kelly asked. Her strokes splashed even more furiously than Violet's.

"I lost him," Hector said. "He went under. Maybe he's gone."

He's not. Violet didn't want to say it though. *He's just going to pop up, any time, any place. He's probably shooting through the water like a shark.*

"If he's walking along the bottom, water resistance should slow him down, right Vi?" Kelly said.

117

"Hopefully." Violet didn't believe that for a second. She paddled harder. "Listen you guys, when we get to the other side, we should make our way north to Anna's cottage. I have a feeling it'll be safer than camp."

"I never thought a crazy cat lady could sound so warm and inviting." Kelly groaned with each stroke.

"Almost two thirds of the way across," Hector said. "You guys can do this."

A powerful jolt from below rocked the canoe. Violet's elbow kissed the water as they wobbled. Her paddle slipped away. She clutched the sides to steady herself. She turned to check on the others just in time to see the crescent curve of Harry's ax erupt through the bottom of the boat between Kelly and Hector. Water boiled around the hot blade.

Hector screamed and backed into Violet's arms. "We're gonna die!" he shouted.

Violet met Kelly's eyes. They pleaded with her, lost and hopeless. Water gushed into the bottom of the boat and sizzled around the ax. Violet's mind raced in desperation. They were too far from either shore. In their haste to get away, they had even forgotten to grab life jackets. Harry was an excellent swimmer, and apparently he didn't have to breathe underwater.

"Nobody's going to die," Violet insisted. She thought back to Hector and herself in the woods earlier. Two of them. One of Harry. *He can only go in one direction.* "I'm going to swim for shore," Violet said. "He's going to come after me. As soon as he does, you two make a break for it. Keep your distance from each other. He can't catch all of us."

Kelly shook her head. "That's crazy."

Violet winked at her. "I'm a good swimmer. It's okay."

"I've never seen you swim," Kelly's voice cracked. "You're lying."

Harry's ax unwedged from the bottom of the boat. The canoe teetered, and more water gushed through the wooden gash. The blade shot up again, making a cross in the same spot. Hector and Kelly backed further apart. Icy water rose around their ankles.

"You're not playing the hero, Violet," Kelly said. She stood. "We all jump. Count of three. Everyone picks a different direction. He can only get one of us."

Violet nodded. She knew she was a terrible swimmer. Harry would come after her.

They each prepared themselves, facing different directions. Kelly counted, "One . . . two . . . three!"

Violet dove into the freezing water. She floundered her way towards the camp shore. *Hector and Kelly will go for the closer side,* she thought. *If I swim for camp, I'm easy prey for Harry. I'll buy them enough time.*

She huffed and struggled across the lake. Waiting for Harry to grab her ankles and pull her under. Or maybe he would just skewer her in the back. One swift stab and that would be it. Maybe she would see her mom.

Violet struggled and kicked frantically. Her arms were so tired from paddling that she could barely lift them. Why wasn't Harry attacking her? Was he toying with her again? She gasped for air and glanced behind her. Had he gone after the other two after all? It was too dark to see.

She searched the water for Harry's glow, but found nothing. No Harry. No wrecked canoe. No Kelly or Hector. Just the shadows of distant pine trees, a swirling sea of stars above, and cold, dark water everywhere else. Her legs were too tired to kick. Her heart pulsed. Vision blurred.

Harry gets the last laugh after all, she thought. Violet's heroics had led her to a watery grave, and Hector and Kelly didn't have much of a chance either. She clung to her remaining bits of strength and took one last deep breath.

Violet clutched her mother's ankh and sank below the surface of Lake Coldwater.

21

Violet coughed up foul-tasting water. A tall shadow pressed down on her sternum. She wanted to scream, but instead hacked up more water. She gagged for air. Her elbows dug into mud.

"She's okay," came Gary's voice. "Thank God! She's going to be fine." A chorus of relieved sighs and hushed chatter surrounded her.

Violet gagged and coughed more. She fidgeted on the murky ground. *I'm on shore,* she thought. *I didn't drown.* Then she processed the fact that Gary was the shadow hovering over her. "Get away from me!" she screamed. "Get away!"

Images of Happy Harry advancing on the bridge, hacking through cabin 28, and sinking the canoe flooded over her. She screamed and struggled. Every time she looked at Gary's face, Harry's jack-o-lantern glow flashed over it.

"Violet, it's okay!" someone shouted.

"You're fine, Violet." Gary put his hand on her shoulder. "Just calm down."

"Don't touch me! Get off me!" She struggled.

"Violet!" the voice to her right said. "You're safe." Kelly placed her hands on Violet's cheeks. "Harry's gone."

Violet calmed herself. "*Gone* gone?"

Kelly smiled weakly but gave no indication one way or the other. Violet hacked up one last volley of scummy water.

Gary took a step back as Violet sat upright. Every muscle in her body ached. Kelly hugged her tight. It only made the pain worse, but she hugged back anyway. "Hector!" she cried suddenly. "Where's Hec--"

"I'm here." Hector kneeled to her left.

Violet couldn't think of a thing to say; she just gave him a big hug too.

"I'm glad you're okay," he said.

She took a moment to process the situation, then turned on Gary. "You've got a lot of explaining to do!" She struggled to her feet and pointed at him. "What exactly do you think--"

"Violet! Violet! Stop!" Hector and Kelly both grabbed her, trying to calm her.

"Violet," Kelly whispered. "Gary saved us. He went after Harry. He pulled you out of the water. He revived you."

Violet was dumbstruck.

Gary nodded. "I think we should talk, Violet," he said under his breath. "Let's keep this situation under control."

Violet nodded.

Gary turned to the crowd of kids behind him and shouted in his up-beat but authoritative tone, "Okay, campers, we've had a serious situation tonight, and the phones are still down. Safety is our *big*--" he gestured wide with both arms, "priority! I want everyone in the cafeteria. Find your buddies, find your bunkmates. We'll have a head count in ten minutes!"

The kids murmured in agreement and started to make their way to the cafeteria. Gary kept a close eye on the crowd, periodically scanning the lake and woods.

Once the other campers were close to the cafeteria, Gary turned back to Violet. "You sure you're okay? Nothing's broken?"

Violet shrugged. "I think I'll be fine once every muscle in my body stops hurting."

Gary nodded. "Okay. Hector and Kelly, find some dry clothes and then head back to the cafeteria with everyone else. Violet, let's go have a chat in my office. We'll get you some clean clothes too. And, uh," he lowered his voice even more, "I'll get you some answers."

Violet followed Gary in a daze. She hadn't even noticed Hector and Kelly break off to join the others. Her instincts started kicking in. Following Gary didn't feel right, but he *had* saved her. It made no sense. *These answers better be good*, she thought.

Back at the main lobby, Gary found Violet a thick wool blanket. He draped it over her shoulders and led her into his office. Violet took a seat and began to dry her arms.

"I should get you a change of clothes and some hot chocolate," Gary said.

"No offense, Gary, but I'd rather have answers now and warmth later." Violet's voice was scratchy from coughing.

"Alright." Gary sat across from her. "This probably won't surprise you, Violet. But I'm a demon hunter."

Violet sighed in frustration. "Why didn't you *tell* me? My dad's the top paranormal investigator in the Western Hemisphere!"

Gary stared in confusion. "I met your dad. I thought he was some kind of professor."

"Well, we don't go broadcasting to the world that we're ghost hunters. People think that's weird," Violet explained.

Gary smiled.

"Which is why you didn't tell me you were a demon hunter. *Duh!* Got it."

Gary nodded. "It's a shame. I would have told your dad to take you home if I knew he'd understand the situation."

"Let's start from the beginning of that situation, Demon Hunter Gary," Violet said.

"I grew up in Coldwater Creek. People here are more open-minded about the supernatural than most. The few who make their homes nearby know better than to wander these woods in the dark. But the company that built this camp . . ."

"Doesn't believe in ghost stories," Violet said. "Big mistake."

Gary nodded. "That wasn't a problem for years, but demons like Happy Harry hunt in cycles. Things get really bad, people die, and the demon goes dormant. Sometimes for a full generation. We knew Camp Coldwater was a problem waiting to happen. So when my contacts here reported increased sightings over the winter, I decided it was time for a homecoming."

"You're here to protect us."

Gary nodded again. "To try, at least."

"No wait!" Violet held up her hands in protest. "That makes no sense. Why not just cancel camp? Tell all the parents to keep their kids home."

"The camp's parent management company would never have gone along with that. Time was running out, and my best bet was to level with the head counselor."

"Michael Heart? The guy who made the good schedule?"

Gary gave a cockeyed glare.

"Uh, sorry. I've been sneaking around your office and your computer and stuff." She smiled awkwardly.

Gary sighed. "That's probably what I would have done in your shoes. I'm sure some of the things I've been doing seem more than a little weird, but hopefully, they're making more sense now."

"Almost," Violet said. "But not really. You fired all the old counselors? You purposefully rearranged the rooms so mean kids would--hey wait! You *paid* the Tuckers and Becky to be bad!"

Gary nodded shamefully.

"Why?"

"The first reason is simple. You see, Violet, we could burn this camp to the ground, and insurance would pay to have it set right back up again next summer. But what's a surefire way to put a stop to this death trap?"

Violet shrugged. "Paying mean kids?"

"Word of mouth. If campers are having a terrible time, they're going to call their parents, and their parents are going to come pick them up. The parents will be enraged, and they'll tell other parents to keep their kids away. Bad word of mouth destroys a business. We hoped the camp would flop years ago, but it was actually loads of fun."

"You went out of your way to make this camp awful? You encouraged jerky kids to pick on nice kids like Hector?" Violet felt a little sick.

"Believe me, it's not what I wanted, but it was a choice between tormented and teased campers . . . or dead ones." Gary stood and took his keys out of his pocket. He crossed the room to the locked closet. "Since you've been snooping around, I assume you found this." He unlocked and opened it, revealing a mounted shotgun on the interior door.

"You think a gun is going to stop Happy Harry?" Violet shook her head.

"It might slow him down, but I was talking about these." He removed a dark red jar and showed it to her. It was labeled "BBQ."

"Barbeque sauce?"

Gary shook his head. He tilted the jar, and Violet watched the syrupy liquid ooze along the glass.

After a moment, it struck her. "Gross! You have *blood* in your closet! Please tell me you weren't serving that at cookouts."

"Relax." Gary replaced the jar. "It's ram's blood. The label's just to throw people off. But it's part of a spell of protection that feeds off negative energy." He reached into the closet again and produced a plank of polished wood, etched with the letters of the alphabet.

"That's a spirit board," Violet said.

"A Ouija board, yes."

"My dad says nothing good ever comes from dabbling in the occult, Gary. You might have made things worse."

"Necessary evil, Violet. Limited time, limited options."

"Let me guess: Sassy and her inverted pentagram necklace were part of this?"

Gary nodded. "Not the friendliest camp counselor, I know, but she's my go-to expert on black magic."

"So part of this spell required kids to be miserable?"

"Happy Harry is drawn to innocence. If I encouraged enough nasty, rotten, bratty behavior, I could make the camp grounds seem unappealing. I didn't think it would work all summer, but it didn't need to. If the phones weren't out, kids' parents would be driving up to get them right now."

Gary took a deep breath and sat back down. He closed his eyes and massaged his temples. "The worst part is all those slacker counselors I hired. Almost all of them bailed when they saw Harry across the lake. Now it's just me and seventy-five kids in a cafeteria."

"Why don't we all just leave?"

"The buses only come for special events. I could shuttle three kids at a time in my four-door sports car. But once I'm gone, no telling who might come strolling back into camp."

Violet had no answer. "I can't believe the phones have been down all night. Are you sure about the cell tower?"

"I can't believe Harry came right onto the grounds." Gary threw up his hands in exasperation. "The spell should have worked. Unless . . ." He eyed Violet suspiciously. "Unless he found an innocent out in the forest and became fixated. Followed them back here." Gary's accusing stare intensified.

Violet's heart sank.

"You went looking for him?"

Violet flushed with embarrassment. She nodded.

"Violet, I'm desperately trying to keep you guys safe, and you actually wandered off to *find* Harry?"

"If I had known . . ." she trailed off. "What about the local woman in the forest," she said, trying to change the subject. "Anna. Do you know her?"

"She's a nut, Violet. Don't listen to her. She thinks she's a Wiccan priestess or something."

"She said she and her husband had beaten Harry before."

"He always comes back. Violet, that woman is unhinged."

"Harry killed her husband. He killed her only child." Violet rubbed her ankh between her thumb and pointer finger. "That would make *me* crazy."

"Harry's a monster, Violet," Gary said. "She shouldn't be living in those woods at all. She shouldn't have been trying to raise a family, knowing he was out there."

"Harry wasn't always a monster, though. The story is true. Just the way you told it to us. Isn't it?"

"Every last word. He was a desperate man in the beginning. Five kids to feed, could barely get himself out of bed in the morning. The Devil is exceptionally tricky, Violet. Harry Hellberg was exactly the kind of person he selects to corrupt."

"I think Anna's cottage is safe," Violet said. "I think she has a different kind of protection at work. Positive energy."

"How do you know?"

"I don't know . . . I could just feel it when I was there."

Gary shook his head. "The woman's loony. And she's *not* safe out there. I have a feeling she'll be seeing her son again. Soon enough."

Violet thought of the way Anna had been drawn to her mother's ankh. How she recognized it as a symbol of something pure. She had a hard time believing Harry could walk right up to Anna's door at any time and claim her.

"I'm sorry, Violet. I don't mean to scare you. I hope I'm wrong for her sake. It's just that I don't want anyone sneaking off the grounds anymore. Deal?"

Violet nodded. "Deal."

"Okay." Gary stood. "I have to check on those kids. Then I'll grab you some dry clothes."

She nodded.

"And then we'll go to the cafeteria together and have some hot tea. Sound good?"

"Yeah, sounds great." Violet smiled. She held out her hand, and Gary shook it. "It's nice to meet the real Gary."

"It's nice to meet a fellow demon hunter." He took his shotgun off the closet door and loaded it. Then he grabbed a box of shells and headed for the lobby. "Sit tight. I won't be long." He shut the door behind him.

Violet took a deep cleansing breath. After a moment, she heard a key turn and a locking sound. Gary had locked the office from the outside.

She stared at the door pensively. There didn't appear to be an interior lock. She calmly crossed the room and tried the knob. It wouldn't budge.

She knocked. "Hey Gary!" she shouted. "You might think that you're just keeping me safe, but this door doesn't unlock from the in--" Suddenly something Gary said resonated in her mind: *The Devil is exceptionally tricky.*

Violet wandered back to Gary's desk. The map with the X was still taped to the wall. Written above the X was the number 12. It wasn't twelve paces, twelve feet, or twelve headstones. It was twelve o'clock. Midnight.

The digital clock on the wall read 9:00 p.m.

Violet's eyes traveled down to the surface of Gary's desk. She fixated on the circle drawn on the current day of the

126

calendar. A white circle. Violet's hand shook as she pushed the keyboard further back to reveal more of the calendar.

Please let me be wrong. Please let me be wrong.

Lined up with the white circle on each week were other circles. Half-black, half-white. More white with just a sliver of black. Leading right up to the full white circle. Anna's words haunted her: *Harry's murderous impulses wax and wane with the moon.*

Gary's desk calendar was a *lunar* calendar, and everything he'd been planning led up to tonight.

22

Violet hoisted Gary's chair as high as she could and slammed it against the office window. She shattered the glass and poked at the shards along the bottom of the frame until it looked safe. She set the chair against the wall and climbed up.

Her muscles ached from running, rowing, and swimming, but she managed to crawl through. She thudded on the ground outside and groaned. *At least I'm getting lots of nice, wholesome exercise at camp,* she thought.

The full, pale moon gleamed behind wisps of cloud. There was no time to lose. She had to get to the cafeteria and warn the other kids.

Her sides split as she raced across camp. As she neared the front of the cafeteria, she noticed chains wrapped around the handles of the main doors, secured by a padlock. The kids had been locked in from the outside. *Gary sure has a funny way of protecting people,* she thought.

Violet crept to the side windows and kept low to the ground. She poked her eyes over the windowsill. In spite of being packed with kids, the dining hall was unsettlingly quiet. Kids slumped over the tables, resting. Some of them talked in hushed voices. Across the hall, Violet spotted a girl crying.

She crawled along until she had a view of the serving trays on the far end. Sassy kept watch with her hands on her hips. A male counselor, pale with dark circles under his eyes, leaned against the back door. *Looks like Gary has a few thugs left in his service,* she thought.

She spied Becky at a nearby table with her face propped up against her fist. Her eyes were sunken beneath her perfect blond bangs. Violet crept closer. "Psst! Becky!"

Becky jumped. Before she could open her mouth, Violet put her finger over her lips. "Shhh!" She whispered, "Where's Gary?"

Becky glanced up at the two counselors to make sure they weren't paying attention. She leaned closer to the cracked window. "Gary left," Becky said. "He had a gun. He said he had something important to do."

"This is not good." Violet struggled to think. "Okay, Becky, you need to--very discretely--find Hector and Kelly and tell them to take a window seat. I need to talk to them."

Becky frowned, dead-eyed.

"Hey, Earth to Becky!" Violet snapped. "Can you please go get my friends, like five minutes ago?"

"Violet," she said. "I'm sorry, but . . ."

"But what?" Violet's stomach churned.

"Gary took them," Becky finally said.

Violet's heart sank.

"He had a shotgun. He told everyone to sit down and shut up. Then he took Hector and Kelly outside."

"Which direction?" Violet asked.

Before Becky could answer, someone grabbed Violet's arms from behind. "You--" came a male voice.

Violet struggled and kicked.

"--were supposed to be waiting--"

She attempted to elbow her attacker in the ribs, but he had her firmly by the upper arms.

"--in the office!"

"Let me go!" Violet shouted.

"Be quiet, and there won't be any trouble," the man said.

Violet thought back to Gary, his shotgun, and Hector and Kelly. *Relax,* she thought. *It's just another one of Gary's stupid counselors. But they might be armed too. If you don't struggle, you won't get hurt.*

The counselor dragged her by the arms towards the back end of the cafeteria. Violet locked eyes with one of the hulking Tucker Triplets, who had stood to look out the window. He raised his eyebrow as if to suggest how pathetic she was.

The counselor pulled her around the back, to an emergency exit. He unlocked the door with a key, yanked her inside, and shoved her against a countertop. "Be still and shut up. We don't want to hurt you kids." The counselor had wiry blond hair and greenish-gray eyes. He showed his yellow teeth.

"Okay," Violet said. "I'm cool. Just let me go sit with my friends."

"Yeah, I don't think so." He unclipped a walkie-talkie from his belt. "Hey Sassy, that Violet kid tried to escape. I've got her in the kitchen."

The radio crackled. "Tie her up and keep her in there. She'll just scare the others. I'll be right there."

"Roger that. Bring rope."

As Wire-Hair clipped his radio back to his belt, Violet rushed him with a sauce pan. She clocked him in the forehead. He stumbled, shouted, and grabbed her wrists. "You little brat!"

"Lemmy, you are pah-thetic!" Sassy stood in the doorway with rope coiled around her arm. Her inverted pentagram necklace dangled over her Camp Coldwater polo.

Violet continued to struggle with Lemmy. "Help!" she screamed. "Everybody get back here!" *There are what? Seventy-something kids at this camp?* She gritted her teeth and kicked Lemmy's shins. *We can take these losers!*

Sassy grabbed Violet's arms from behind while Lemmy held her still. Sassy secured her wrists with tight bonds. "Sorry, sweetie," she said. "Business is business."

She patted Violet's cheek. Then she turned to Lemmy. "Get out there and help Chad keep watch. Those brats make me nervous."

Lemmy rubbed his forehead as he left.

"Okay, Sassy," Violet said. "I think I've actually got most of this pieced together. But indulge me. What the heck do *you* get from sacrificing a camp full of kids to a psycho-demon?"

Sassy fingered her inverted pentagram and paced the kitchen. "We all had our reasons for helping Gary. Some of it was money. Some of it was blackmail. A lot of us bailed before the full moon, as you can see. No big deal. They wouldn't have had the guts for what comes next."

"Which would be?"

"Embracing the cleansing fires of sacrifice." She took a butcher knife off the wall and swayed it back and forth in the air.

"*Human* sacrifice," Violet said. "I get it. You're *all* insane. But I'd love to know why."

"I've been a practicing witch since I was your age, kid, and one thing I know about magic is that you gotta give big to get big."

"Isn't that what the gambler says before he gets eaten by the loan shark?" Violet asked.

Sassy rolled her eyes. "Cute. Whatever Gary's risks might be, I *know* I stand to profit. And I'm not talking money. I mean luck, power, influence, charisma. Dark beings move the world, and when we offer them blood, they are most generous in their rewards."

Violet stared blankly for a moment. Once it was clear that Sassy was finished, she burst into laughter.

"What?" Sassy asked. "What's so funny?"

Violet laughed harder. The ropes dug into her sides, and she gasped for breath.

"Stop it!" Sassy snapped. "Nothing's funny about being sacrificed by a servant of the dark one!"

Violet gasped. "I'm sorry. I'm sorry. It's not funny. It's not. I just . . ." She cracked up again.

Sassy pointed her knife. "Stop laughing!"

"Okay, okay, okay." Violet calmed down. "It's not funny: *you* are."

Sassy glared.

"You're acting like you're this powerful witch, but it sounds like you learned all of this from movies or something." Violet chuckled some more.

Sassy's face burned bright red. "I am a dark witch of the highest order!"

"No, no, no, no." Now Violet was irritated. "Let's get this straight. There's Wicca: a life-affirming religion that draws on pagan ritual and encourages a deep connection to nature. And then there's *worshipping Satan*! You are the latter. So stop acting like you know what you're talking about and admit that you're in *way* over your head."

"I'm not in over my--"

"People who make deals with demons always get in over their heads," Violet snapped. "Same goes for people who make deals with people who make deals with demons *for* them."

"Gary's my link to Harry's dark energies, it's true. He needed me to channel the spells that manipulated the camp's upper management. Fairly low-level stuff, but it helped us take control and prepare our offering."

Violet groaned. "There are so many deals going on at this camp, I doubt even Gary can keep it all straight!"

Sassy glared. "You don't have to keep it straight, kid. You're just blood. Meat to be consumed by ever-living darkness--"

"Stop it, Sassy! You're not powerful. You're just another grownup, ex-Goth poser with a chintzy inverted pentagram she bought at a souvenir shop in Salem, Massachusetts."

Sassy's jaw dropped. "How did you know I bought--?"

"Please! It's Mecca for wannabe witches. You're not going to be rewarded. But you *are* going to be an accessory to a huge mass murder unless you come to your senses, let me out, and help me stop this!" Violet shouted.

Sassy turned away. "What do you know?"

"More than you, apparently," Violet said.

"Yeah?" Sassy turned around. "Well, it just so happens I *do* know a thing or two about ritual sacrifice. And before the fun starts here, it starts at the cemetery with one boy and one girl. Guess which ones?"

Violet fought back tears. Hector and Kelly.

"Show a little respect, and die with dignity."

"Saaaaaaaasssssy!" a deep voice grinded through the kitchen door.

Sassy glanced around in surprise.

"I have come for you!"

Sassy's lip quivered. "Lemmy?"

"Saaaaaaaaaaaassssy!"

Violet shook her head somberly. "That doesn't sound like Lemmy to me."

Sassy quaked. "D-dark lords?"

"Happy Harry has come to claim you!" the voice grated.

"No!" she shouted. "No, no! I served you well!"

The kitchen door burst open and slammed against the wall. A hulking shadow stood in the doorframe. Sassy screamed.

"Bow to him, Sassy!" Violet shouted. "Bow to him, and he'll spare you!"

Sassy fell to her knees, hyperventilating. She dropped her knife and placed her hands on the floor. "Spare me," she stammered. "Oh please, oh please."

The shadow crossed the kitchen, grabbed Violet's sauce pan off the counter, and whacked Sassy over the head. She collapsed, unconscious.

"Okay," Violet said. "I'm impressed. Not just that you're here, but at that performance too. I'd give a standing ovation but," she wiggled her bound arms behind her back, "you know."

Two more Tuckers appeared in the doorway. "Chad and Lemmy are down for the count, Trent. Now what?"

Trent removed his ghost mask and pulled back the hood of his costume. "Not sure." He untied Violet's bonds and helped her up.

Violet stood and stretched. "Not that anyone's asking me, but I say, tie up these three counselors and see if one of them has a cell phone. Call the cops and get them out here ASAP. What time is it?"

"Pushing ten," Trent said.

"That doesn't give Hector and Kelly enough time," Violet thought aloud. "I have to stop Gary."

"We don't know where he is," Brent, or possibly Brant, said.

"*I* know." Violet shoved her way out the back exit.

Trent called to her from the doorway, "Hey, Violet!"

She turned.

"I didn't know that Gary was . . . this nuts, you know?"

Violet nodded. "Just keep everyone safe. If you get ahold of the cops, tell them Happy Gary's north of the lake. If they're locals, they'll know the place."

23

The bright circle of the moon lit the way as Violet struggled down the forest path. Crickets screeched. Her sides split. Her knees ached. She realized ten minutes into her walk that if she had had half a brain she would have brought a flashlight. But there was no turning back. Every second counted.

She forced herself to keep putting one foot in front of the other. The walk seemed to take so much longer than the one she'd made that morning. And she had no idea what time it was. No idea how close she might be to the north bend of the lake.

Finally, her legs gave up. She collapsed at the side of the trail and rested her head in her arms.

Five minutes, she thought. *Five minutes, and I keep moving.* But Hector and Kelly were out there. Every second could cost them their lives. *I don't deserve five minutes.* She attempted to stand, but her muscles wouldn't listen.

All day she had been fighting for her life. And every time she thought she was on empty, she found some last spark to keep going. Where was that spark now?

She squeezed her mother's ankh. The shrill symphony of crickets vibrated across the forest floor.

I need you, Mom, Violet prayed. *More than ever.* All she wanted was to lie on the ground and rest her eyes. She knew better.

People who are exhausted don't "rest their eyes." They pass out! She forced her eyes open. Moonlight seared her vision.

"Mom, please help me," she said. "I can't stop now. I could never live with myself."

Now was the time in any good story when Violet's mom would come back to her. Would visit her and protect her. Would whisper just the right words of encouragement in her ears. She wanted that so badly.

But all she heard were crickets.

Every other week something fantastical crossed the path of the Black family. Ghosts, demons, curses. Ever since Mom died, Violet and her dad had an unspoken expectation. *We see dead people on a regular basis. Why can't we see Mom? Where is she? Why wouldn't she let us know she's okay?*

She'd heard her dad give the same speech countless times to grieving friends. "The afterlife is mysterious. Some ghosts have unfinished business. Others lived exceptional lives, and their time among us is over."

Violet recalled a story her dad had told of a woman whose husband contacted her from the other side. The man's spirit had appeared in a bright light. He had struggled to speak, as if once he had crossed far enough into the light, it was impossible to send a message. It took tremendous strength and will power for spirits to do it. And it was likely they would only do it if it was extremely important.

After Mom died, Dad didn't tell any of those stories. Maybe he didn't believe them anymore. And why should he? Mom had lots of unfinished business. She had a husband and daughter whom she loved. A daughter who had a million questions for her. *A daughter who needs her right now,* she thought.

Crickets. Nothing but crickets chirping under the moon.

Violet cried. She wanted her mom. She wanted her dad. She wanted someone, anyone to come help her. But it was just her and a forest full of insects.

She took a stilted breath, and got back on her hands and knees. She groaned, cried, and hoisted herself to her feet. She dried her eyes. And kept walking. One foot in front of the other.

Step by step. Tree by tree. No haunted forest, no ax murdering psycho, and no amount of pain was going to stop the daughter of Vivian and Dorian Black.

She trudged on. "I didn't face down a demon, nearly drown, and endure a week of the worst summer camp on Earth just to give up," she growled under her breath.

Finally, she rounded the edge of the lake and saw the clearing. Fire pits flickered around the site of the Hellberg cemetery. A tall shadow stood with a long, thin object resting over his shoulder.

24

Violet crept through the tall grass. Gary stood with his back to her, his shotgun propped over one shoulder. Kelly's and Hector's arms and legs were bound. They sat against Helen Hellberg's headstone.

Gary had prepared five blazing fire pits, spaced in an even circle around the graves. *Five points,* Violet thought, *a downward star. He's started the ritual sacrifice. He must just be waiting for the executioner.*

Fortunately, the crickets and the crackling flames drowned out the sound of Violet's footfalls in the dry field. Gary's back was turned to her. She positioned herself just a few feet away.

Now what? Violet doubted she could wrestle the gun away from Gary. She inched closer until she felt the heat of the southern facing bonfire. Extra lumber lay in a pile within arm's reach.

A fleeting look of recognition crossed Kelly's face. Violet nodded at her. *Come on, Kelly,* she thought. *I could use a distraction.*

"What time is it?" Kelly asked.

"Why do you care?" Gary said.

"Because I want to know when this will all be over."

"I'd rather keep you in suspense." Gary pointed his shotgun with one arm at the both of them. "Just remember: I can end this any time I want."

Violet kept low. She crawled forward and found a long, thin piece of wood from Gary's pile. She held the far end in the nearby bonfire until it caught.

"If you were going to shoot us, you would have already," Kelly said.

"Kelly," Hector groaned. "Be quiet. You're just gonna make him mad."

"Listen to the shrimp, Kelly." Gary took a few steps forward. He pressed the barrel of his gun against Kelly's head. "You don't want to make me angry."

Violet's heart nearly stopped. But Gary stood still. Kelly was right. Gary *wasn't* going to kill them. He needed them alive. More pieces of Gary's story were fitting together. She held her makeshift torch off the ground and crept closer.

Hector gasped as he spotted her, but Gary didn't hear. Violet waited until he pointed the gun back at the ground, then she held her flame against Gary's shirt.

Flannel ignited. Gary twisted in surprise. He dropped his shotgun and screamed as he attempted to pat out the flames on his back. He tripped and fell.

Violet tossed her burning lumber onto Gary. He shouted and rolled in the dirt.

Violet grabbed Gary's shotgun off the ground.

Gary's shirt was charred, but he'd managed to snuff out the flames. He cautiously stood, arms raised. Violet kept the barrel of the gun fixed on him.

"Stay back," Violet said.

"Okay, easy, Violet, easy." Gary inched forward. "You got me, okay. It's over."

"I said back!" Violet shouted.

"You don't want to shoot me, kid. You've never held a gun in your life."

Violet's arms shook. "Don't be so sure."

"It's not so hard to know." Gary stepped forward.

Violet tilted the gun at Gary's knee. She readied her trigger finger.

"The safety's on." Gary lurched forward and tackled Violet. She struggled to keep the gun. Gary's hands fumbled along the sides of the weapon. He pushed the barrel towards Violet's head. Behind her, the fire pit scorched her neck.

He's bluffing, Violet reminded herself. *He won't shoot you.* She groaned. Strained to keep her grip. *Won't burn you.* She worked the barrel of the gun between them.

Gary growled. He started to pry Violet's fingers off the barrel. The shotgun was aimed directly between them. Right at the moon. Violet squeezed the trigger.

The shot echoed. Violet rolled to one side and allowed Gary's full strength to propel him, arms first, into the bonfire.

Gary howled and reared back immediately. His gun remained amid the kindling, engulfed in flame. Violet crawled back to Helen Hellberg's grave, her ears ringing. She worked quickly to untie Kelly's arms. Once Kelly was free, she glanced back to find Gary cursing, attempting to free his searing-hot weapon from the fire pit.

She turned back to help Kelly free Hector. "Listen," she said. "As soon as Hector's free, we all make our way to--"

Gary snatched her from behind, smelling like burned cotton. "Congratulations, Violet Black!" He pinned her arms behind her, pulled her back, and held a knife against her throat. "You are officially the most obnoxious camper to ever grace the shores of Lake Coldwater!" Gary's arms were splotched with bright red burns, but his grip remained iron tight.

"Run, you guys!" Violet screamed. "Get out of here!"

"Nobody's going anywhere!" Gary shouted.

Kelly and Hector froze. The bonfires cast angular shadows against the tall grass.

"Good. Just like that. Hands in the air where I can see them, or we'll see if your gal pal bleeds purple."

They each raised their arms.

"He's not going to kill me," Violet said confidently.

"Don't be so sure," Gary growled.

"If you could kill kids, you'd have let me drown. But no. You made a *deal* didn't you? You owe Happy Harry innocent souls. And if campers drown in the lake, get shot, or get their throats cut, they don't count towards your quota, do they?"

"Well!" Gary laughed derisively. He pushed the blade into her neck ever so slightly. "Aren't you *smart*, Ms. Black!"

"You almost had me, Gary! Quite the improv show in your office. But you slipped up. The second you locked me in, your story stopped adding up. My dad has been telling me for *years* that real ghost hunters don't dabble in the occult. Ouija boards and ram's blood and curses fueled by negative energy? Even in dire situations, those are bad ideas."

"And why's that, smarty-pants?"

"Because when you deal with dark forces, there'll always be a price to pay. It made me think you were *already* paying yours back. Happy Harry made a deal with the Devil, then *you* made a deal with him? For what? Power? Money?"

Gary remained silent.

"No, not you. You're different from your junior counselor goons, aren't you? What is it that made you so desperate that you'd offer up a bunch of innocent kids? What is it that you're bargaining for?"

"His life!" a woman shouted nearby.

Gary turned, keeping Violet firm against his chest.

Anna stared them down with a readied longbow. Her green cloak flowed in the summer wind. She drew an arrow and aimed at Gary. "Let the girl go, son. These children don't have anything to do with us."

"Son?" Hector shouted. "Gary is your son!"

"Witch!" Gary hissed. "You think you can stop this, you deranged old bat? He'll come for you too. He'll finish his job."

"He won't be done until every last one of us is gone." Anna shook her head. "You're only making it worse. Bringing more shame into our family."

"Okay! Time out!" Hector shouted. "Will somebody *please* explain what is going on?"

"I will," Violet said. "You see, on top of being a total psycho, Gary's also the *grandson* of a total psycho. It took me a minute to realize, but when I said Anna's child had been killed by

Harry, Gary referred to the child as a 'son.' But I'd never said he was a boy. Gary also said Harry had *five* kids to feed. But I knew there were only *four* extra headstones here.

"And Gary's spell of protection? Ram's blood? Ouija boards? Negative energy from sad kids? That wasn't meant to help us. It was his way of *breaking* the enchantments his mother had already placed over camp. Anna wasn't ashamed about the son she'd failed to protect . . ."

"I was ashamed of the man he grew into . . . after I saved him." Anna's arrow remained fixed on Gary. "After his father gave his life to protect us." Her tears glinted in the flickering firelight. "Let these children go, Gary. Let that be your final act of redemption."

"Don't count on it, Mother." Gary tightened his grip on Violet. "You see kids, the truth is Happy Harry kills his descendants. True, all the innocent campers got Gramps riled up summer after summer, but at the end of the day, the Hellberg-Matthews clan is what he keeps coming back for. Because this old witch just *won't die!*"

"Gary . . ." Anna pleaded.

"And when she had a baby--thinking she was going to have a happy family in the big woods--she just provided another victim for old Grandpa."

"I didn't know he would keep coming back." Anna's hands trembled. Her arrow shook. "Please let the girl go. Don't make me stop you."

"Wherever I went, whatever I did, I knew he would come. Some dark night on some lonely old road. I couldn't hide from him. But little miss ghost hunter was right. I *could* make a deal. Seventy-five innocent souls, wrapped up in a neat little package." He twisted Violet's arms. "It should have been a smooth transaction, except *you* and your *junior mystery side-kicks* keep throwing me curveballs!"

"You're not going to kill Violet, Gary," Kelly said. "She's one of your seventy-five. You just said it. So let her go already."

"In a minute," Gary whispered. "It's almost midnight. And Grandpa's never late."

Violet realized the crickets had stopped chirping. Wind rustled the grass, and "Hall of the Mountain King" whistled over the trees.

Gary whistled along.

25

An arrow impaled Gary's shoulder with a sickening *SHUNK*! Gary screamed. His arm went limp. The knife fell at Violet's feet.

"Run, children!" Anna shouted.

Violet elbowed Gary in the stomach, shoved him into the tall grass, and raced to Anna. Hector and Kelly joined her. Anna grabbed Violet's arm with one hand and clutched her longbow with the other. "I said *run*!"

"Run where?" Violet said. "We don't know where Harry's coming from."

"Just get away from this spot!" Anna ushered them towards the trail to camp, but Violet resisted.

Kelly tugged her arm. "Violet, come on! Let's get as far away as possible!"

As Violet faced the path, her eyes met Harry's jack-o-lantern glow.

"Down!" Violet tugged Kelly back. Harry's ax swiped past their heads. The glowing blade made a white hot streak in the air.

"Away!" Three of Anna's arrows whizzed over their heads and lodged in Harry's stomach, side, and shoulder. He wailed and stumbled. The three kids gathered behind Anna while she readied another shot.

Harry leaned on his ax. He struggled to yank each arrow from his torso.

"Witch!" Gary grimaced as he wrenched the arrow from his shoulder. He stumbled to his feet. "You can try until you're one-hundred-and-twenty years old." He snapped the arrow and tossed it. "You'll *never* kill him! You're wasting your time!"

Happy Harry pulled the final arrow from his torso and stood.

"Better to fight an impossible battle than give in to wickedness." Anna let another arrow fly. Harry deflected it with the broad side of his ax. She shot two more, and he sliced them midair, sending burning halves sputtering into the grass. Harry laughed his low, grating laugh. Smoke rose from the tall grass. He twisted his ax and swiped through a patch of dry prairie, fanning and fueling the fire.

Anna frantically loaded two more arrows. All eyes were on Harry when Gary tackled her from the side. "You're not taking this away from me, Mother!"

Violet, Hector, and Kelly wrestled Gary by the arms and dragged him off. But not before Violet heard a loud snap. Anna screamed and held her wrist. Her longbow lay in the dirt. A wall of fire spread beside them. Fire circled the surrounding long grass, confining them to the Hellberg burial site.

Between the prairie fire and the five glowing pits, the cemetery blazed brighter than daylight. There was only one way out now: straight through Happy Harry.

"Stones!" Anna screamed. "Moon!"

"Go ahead and scream!" Gary raved. "You've had this coming!"

"Shut! Up!" Kelly punched Gary in his arrow wound, and he doubled over in pain.

"Moon." Anna reached at them. "Stones . . ."

"Moonstones?" Violet shook her head. "What about moonstones?"

Anna grimaced as she attempted to sit up. She fell back to the ground. ". . . will stop him! The heart . . . or the head."

"Look out!" Hector shouted. Harry rushed them, slashing at the air. The three kids darted in different directions. Violet tripped on a headstone and fell face first into the grass.

She struggled to sit up. A flat, white, object doubled in her blurred vision. It was an arrowhead, lying nearby: the arrow Gary had snapped and tossed.

Hector attempted to pull her to her feet. "Get up, Violet! Kelly, run!"

Happy Harry had become fixated on Anna and Gary, his two descendants.

"Precious wood!" Anna panted. "Buried in sacred soil!"

Gary lifted his blistered, bloody arm and pointed towards Violet and Hector. "We had a deal! Those are your offerings! Plenty more where they came from!"

"Sacred soils, consecrated by innocent flesh. White stones soaked in blessed water!" Anna chanted.

"Violet, move!" Hector screamed.

"You go, Hector. I'll be right there." Violet got to her knees. She plucked the arrowhead off the ground. *White stone,* she thought. The image of the stones soaking in Anna's cottage flashed back. *These aren't ordinary arrows.*

"I am not leaving without you," Hector said. "Not again! We stick together!"

Harry held his burning ax close to Anna's throat. Soft white light shined through the holes in his torso.

"Hey, Harry!" Violet shouted. "Gary's right! We're the main course."

Harry's eight eyes burned at her.

Violet clutched the arrowhead behind her back. "So start with me." She said under her breath, "Get out of here, Hector."

"Forget it," he said.

"Run, children!" Anna shouted.

Harry advanced.

"You'd better have a plan here," Hector whispered.

"I know we can't outrun you, Harry. But I was thinking . . ."

Harry's dagger-eyes smoldered.

"If Gary can make a deal with you, so can I."

Harry stopped in his tracks, just a few feet away. He tilted his head. His face blazed. His hands clutched the twisted stem of his ax.

"I see I've got your attention," Violet said. "The Devil promised you happiness, but he never gave you *real* happiness, did he? Just twisted euphoria. It's like being on drugs, isn't it?"

Harry stared blankly.

"You wanted peace. The strength to move on and raise your children. Now your family is in ruin. But it wasn't your fault, was it? It was the Devil's lies."

Harry stared.

"So here's *my* deal. You spare all seventy-five kids and your daughter. Return to wherever it is that you go when you're dormant. And in exchange, my father and I will do everything we can to free you from your servitude. Someday."

Harry's face gleamed.

Gary snickered.

"Violet," Hector whispered. "We tried this, remember? I don't think you can reason with Happy Harry."

"What do you think of that deal, Grandpa?" Gary laughed harder. Harry's dark laughter joined in.

"It's okay, Hector," Violet said. "Just follow my lead."

"What?"

"Now!" Violet stabbed Harry under the ribcage with the arrowhead. "You can't reason with him, but you sure can surprise him. Eat sacred stone, pumpkin-head!" She twisted the arrow further in.

Harry gave an unearthly growl. Hector charged, and together they toppled him. Hector pulled Violet back. Harry swiped at the sky. He snarled and chopped one of his children's markers, sending chunks of stone into the air.

Harry fished into his guts with a long, tapered hand. He screamed in agony as he clutched, untwisted, and removed the glowing white stone. His fingers smoked. He tossed the arrowhead into the fiery grass. Then he turned back on Violet and Hector. For the first time, he wasn't smiling.

"Hey, Mr. Happy!" Kelly shouted from where Anna had fallen. She had a holy arrow strung up in the longbow. "Why the long face?" She shot her arrow through Harry's left arm. He hissed in pain and dropped his ax.

Kelly fumbled on the ground for another arrow. Violet rushed to help her, but Harry grabbed the back of her shirt. He tossed her to the ground and wrapped his fingers around her neck.

Violet kicked and screamed. The heat from Harry's face burned her skin. His claws dug into her throat.

"Let her go!" Hector hoisted the twisted, glowing ax and shoved it deep into Harry's back. Harry screamed and reached behind him. Blue flames spread over his coat.

Hector helped Violet to her feet. Harry groped over his shoulders for the handle of his ax. As he screamed, fire shot from his mouth and eyes.

Kelly had another arrow ready.

"Aim for the head!" Violet shouted.

"I need a clear shot!" Kelly called out.

Violet's heart pounded. She dove forward and wrapped her arms around the gnarled ax handle protruding from Harry's back. She attempted to steady his writhing body, but Harry was too strong. He dragged her through dirt and grass. Hector grabbed the handle from the other side. Between the two of them, they held him in one spot, but they couldn't keep him completely still.

"Now or never, Kelly!" Hector said.

The glowing point of an arrow shot through the back of Harry's head.

"Bull's-eye!" Kelly shouted.

White fire ignited Harry's skull. His screams skyrocketed into a horrible shrill sound unlike anything Violet had ever heard. Hector and Violet raced to Kelly's side. They watched as ashen white light spread over Harry's skeletal frame.

"No, no, no!" Gary stumbled towards Harry. "You're not giving up that easy!" He reached for the shaft of the arrow sticking through his grandfather's blazing skull and attempted to pull it free, but his hand recoiled from the heat. "Come on!" he screamed. "You're worthless!"

Harry's arms snapped up and grabbed Gary by the shirt. Before Gary could even scream, both Hellberg men incinerated in a white flash.

The fire in the grass died out. Only faint traces of smoke lingered in the night.

Violet helped Anna to her feet. "Your wrist . . ."

"Sprained," she said. "I can take care of it."

"I don't doubt it," Violet said. She stared back at the spot where Gary and Harry had vanished. A black mark scorched the earth beside the headstones. "What Gary said about Harry coming back for his descendants . . ."

"He won't be back," Anna said. "That arrow will keep him away far longer than I'll last in this world."

"Then it's over."

Anna nodded. "Three generations of evil. And it ends with me."

Violet placed her hand on Anna's shoulder. "You've always done the right thing. I think you've earned some peace."

Anna tried to smile. "Perhaps." She wrapped her arm in her cloak and made a makeshift sling. "I would see you children safely back, but I don't think the police would understand my part in this."

"Man incinerated by sacred flames while being clutched by demon never looks good in a police report," Violet pondered. "We'll just say Gary dragged these two out here, set a fire, and left. I found you guys, and we made our way back."

Hector and Kelly nodded in agreement.

"Very well." The old woman touched the ankh around Violet's neck. "Godspeed to all of you. You make your mother proud."

Violet fought back tears. "Thank you."

Anna sang softly to herself as she made her way around the other side of the lake. A sweet, low tune that was soon drowned out by a chorus of crickets.

Violet collapsed onto Hector and Kelly's shoulders. "I don't suppose you guys are willing to carry me home?"

26

The police arrived later that night. By the following morning, Gary's satanic junior counselors were behind bars, and the previous summer's team of friendly professionals had been reinstated.

Michael Heart, the original head counselor, turned out to be a really nice guy. He gave Violet and Kelly advanced archery lessons. Not that Kelly really needed them. He also respected the campers' newfound hatred for ghost stories, only telling corny jokes around the fires at night.

The campers all agreed that Gary had been dressing as Happy Harry. Hector and Kelly hated that the entire week of strange events had been pinned on a single deranged counselor, but Violet assured them it was the best "on the record" explanation.

What mattered was that once the camp was no longer being run by the satanic descendant of a supernatural ax murderer, they all got the nice normal summer the Camp Coldwater brochure had promised.

The sun burned bright on the last day of camp. The air reeked of rubber hotdogs. Kids laughed, teased, screamed, and sang. Camp Coldwater was back to normal.

Hector chucked a rock at the lake, and it plummeted through the surface. "I'm never going to be able to skip these." He sighed and sat next to Violet.

"You win some; you lose some," she said.

He smiled wide. Violet could barely believe he was the same kid from six weeks ago, screaming and leaping for his shoes in a tree.

"I'm gonna miss you," he said.

"Me too." Kelly gave her a friendly punch on the opposite arm.

"All right, all right." Violet held up her hands. "I have to confess, I really hate the whole goodbye thing. So let's just all agree that we live in a world of email, texts, and webcams, and we'll all stay in touch. No matter where we end up."

Kelly smiled. "Deal."

"Plus I still owe Hector a computer," Violet said. "I'll make it happen. I promise."

Hector shrugged. "No worries. I found over $400 in Trent Tucker's dresser drawer after they went home."

"That's dirty money, Hector," Violet said. "But I'm sure you'll put it to good use. If I ever need research assistance, you know I'm emailing you." She held out her fist, and Hector bumped it. "You rock."

"Violet!" a familiar voice called out. "Violet Black!"

Violet sprang to her feet. She raced through the picnic tables. Her dad scanned the grounds, a hand cupped over his eyes to block the sun. She leapt into his arms.

"Hello darling!" He squeezed her in a hug. "I take it this means camp was a hellhole, and you're ready to go home?"

"Yes to the hellhole, technically. But I *did* have fun."

"You're not going to give me grief about that counselor who went mad? I understand a lot of parents pulled their children out early."

"All the cool kids stayed," she said.

"Well I want to hear all about it." He sat at a picnic table. "But first, I had a rather exhilarating summer myself."

Violet sat next to him and held his arm. "Do tell, Professor Black."

"It was dangerous to be sure, but here I am in one piece. We found the most wicked infestation of poltergeists in Sussex." His eyes sparkled whenever he talked about work. "You wouldn't believe the tenacity, the pure malevolence."

"I could try and imagine," Violet said. "But I'm sure I wouldn't do it justice."

"I'd be delighted to fill you in on the drive home. But long story short, I have exciting news. Cambridge, as you know, is very hush-hush about our studies. But they have a sizable allocation of funds for parapsychology which the board looks the other way on. And, well, their representative was most impressed."

Violet frowned. "You're getting a job in London?" She had known she wasn't going to be seeing Hector and Kelly again soon. But London? "Daddy, I made some new friends, and I was hoping that we would at least stay in the States. So that maybe they could visit or something."

"Well that's lovely, Violet. Where do they live?"

"Wisconsin. But if we're all the way in London--"

"This is the best part, Violet." He put his hand on her shoulder. "I'm getting a huge grant for independent investigation. I'll be traveling. You'll travel with me sometimes, depending on school. But we can live literally anywhere."

"Really?" she asked.

He nodded. "I had been thinking upstate New York . . . but I'm open-minded." He cleaned his glasses on his shirt. "Small Wisconsin town. Sounds lovely." He kissed her on the head.

Violet gave him a big kiss on the cheek then raced back to the lake. "Hey guys!" she screamed. "I'm moving to Wisconsin!"

* * *

After the final barbeque, Violet said her goodbyes. She swapped emails, phone numbers, and addresses with Hector and Kelly. Her dad was going to do his best to find a place near their school. It wasn't a guarantee, but Violet had a good feeling. The sky was dark orange with sunset as they drove under the metal "COLDWATER" archway. Violet whistled to herself

"Hall of the Mountain King?" her father asked. "Do they teach classical music at this camp? Perhaps I chose the right one after all."

Violet smiled. "It's sort of part of this ghost story they tell."

"Really? I'd like to hear it." They turned onto the darkening forest road.

"Okay," Violet said. "But I want to hear about the poltergeists in Sussex too. You first."

ABOUT THE AUTHOR

Kevin Folliard is a Chicago area author whose works include the acclaimed videogame parody *Press Start* films and web cartoons. His published fiction includes the scary stories collection *Christmas Terror Tales* and the dark fantasy novel *Jake Carter & the Nightmare Gallery*.

ABOUT THE COVER ARTIST

J.T. Molloy is a Chicago area artist and post production editor. Recent works include *Christmas Terror Tales* and the action adventure graphic novel *The Sapphire Spectre*.

Available by the same author . . .

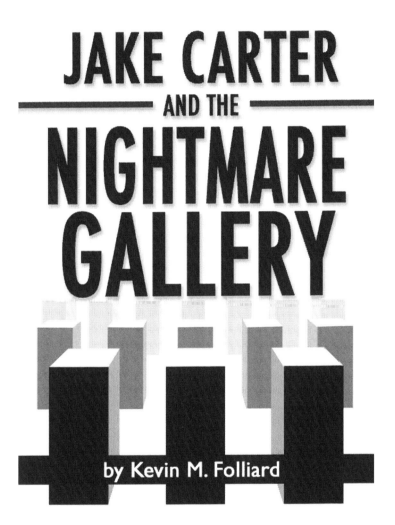

JAKE CARTER
— AND THE —
NIGHTMARE
GALLERY

by Kevin M. Folliard

24265903R00085

Made in the USA
Charleston, SC
21 November 2013